ALL BECAUSE OF YOU

A WALKER BEACH ROMANCE

LINDSAY HARREL

Blue Aster PRESS

For Nancy Harrel and Kristin Walker
Thank you for being mothers to me when mine was no longer here.
Your love and acceptance of me as a daughter has meant the world.
I love you both so very much!

CHAPTER 1

Two weeks. She only had to endure Walker Beach for two weeks.

Madison Price gripped the steering wheel as she parallel parked in front of the quaint blue and yellow storefront on Main Street. At first glance, Hole-in-the-Wall Hardware looked much the same as it always had.

But one thing was glaringly different from the last time she'd been here—Aunt Chrissy wasn't.

An ache pierced her heart, but Madison shook it away. She pulled her phone from her purse and shot off the text she'd considered sending during the entire four-hour drive north from Los Angeles. *I want to make an offer on the Dalton Street House. Asking price, like we discussed. Thanks.*

She hoped her realtor in Oregon would respond soon. Not that Madison didn't have plenty to distract her in the meantime. But it would be nice to have a home to go along with the assistant librarian job she'd start in just fifteen days.

Madison cast another wary glance at the store to her right, climbed from the packed-to-the-hilt car, and tucked her phone into the back pocket of her jeans. She probably should have dropped off her stuff at Aunt Chrissy's house, but something had compelled her to come here first. Dodging a few stray passersby, Madison unlocked the front door and stepped into the darkened store.

A small bit of light filtered in from the large front window, enough for her to make out the shadowed rows of hardware supplies and the hulking oak desk where she'd seen her aunt countless times, cashing out Walker Beach patrons and dishing out a larger-than-life smile. The place still smelled of wood dust and lemon, a mixture so familiar that she hadn't realized she'd missed it until now.

Madison reached for the light switch, but as she did, the back door creaked open and something clattered to the ground. Even from the front of the store, she could hear the wooden floorboards in the back groan and settle as someone walked across them.

Her breath stuttered. Was a thief taking advantage of the relatively quiet day on Main Street and the store that had been empty for more than four months? Walker Beach, California, had always been synonymous with safety, but a lot could have changed in the ten years since Madison had lived here.

Tiptoeing to the closest shelf where the hammers once had been stored, she fumbled along until she gripped a solid wooden handle. As quietly as she could, she crept toward the back, where someone was making quite a racket. If it were a thief, they were not a stealthy one.

After advancing through the front room, she tucked herself behind the desk and peered around the corner into the small kitchen that served as a break room. Her eyes first caught sight of the open back door and the sand and ocean just beyond. Then her gaze roamed the room, landing on a pair of legs. What the . . .

A man was lying on his back, his head stuck underneath the

break room sink, a wrench in his hand. And he was humming. Loudly.

OK, so most likely not a thief, unless there was some black-market demand for plumbing parts she didn't know about. But for some reason the heightened speed of her pulse continued. Madison stepped fully into the room. "What are you doing in my store?"

The man surged into a sitting position, his head smacking the top of the cabinet along the way. The wrench hurtled to the ground as he covered his face with his hands, groaning.

Sucking in a breath, Madison rushed forward. "Oh, sorry. I didn't mean for that to happen."

But at that moment, the man lowered his hand, and Madison couldn't help the gasp that fell from her lips.

What was *he* doing here?

Evan Walsh was as handsome now as he'd been during their senior year of high school. Instead of the tousled hair that had always made him appear as if he'd just rolled out of bed, he sported a casual blond brush-up. A defined jawline and full stubble had replaced sparse whiskers, and his wider shoulders gave way to crafted arms that peeked out from the rolled sleeves of his blue dress shirt. The only thing that hadn't changed about him were those piercing aqua eyes, the ones that had inspired more than one female at Walker Beach High to compose a silly love poem.

And yet, the sight of him still clenched Madison's stomach. "I asked what you're doing in my store."

"*Your* store?" He studied her for a moment, eyebrows puckered in confusion, until his eyes widened. "Oh, wow, you must be Madison."

He made it sound like he had no idea who she was. As if he hadn't spent months writing her pen pal letters that had ended up being a cruel joke. Evan Walsh, of all people, should have known her name.

Or maybe he only remembered the one he'd invented for her.

"Yeah, I'm Madison." *Not* Lizard Lady.

Evan stared at her, a grin curling around his lips. "And, Madison, tell me, what exactly are you planning to do with that?" His amused gaze traveled to her hand, and she looked down.

Instead of the hammer she'd intended to grab in defense, she'd snagged a plunger.

She set it down onto the small table behind her as her cheeks reddened. "I thought you were a thief."

"And so you said, 'Hey, I'll plunge the guy to death?'" Evan stood and brushed off his beige slacks, chuckling.

Madison backed up at his sudden nearness. "Well? Why are you here?"

"Your aunt asked me to keep an eye on things until you came back or sold the place. Of course, if I'd known it would be nearly five months, I'd have asked for double what she was paying me." At her lack of reply, he tilted his head, his smile disappearing. "Hey, it's just a joke. Are you OK?"

"Why would she have asked *you* for help?" Her aunt knew how Madison had felt about him and his dumb friends. Not that it mattered anymore.

Evan rubbed the back of his neck, a guarded look on his face. "We became close during the last few years." He cleared his throat. "I'm really sorry for your loss, by the way."

Heat flashed at the back of Madison's eyes, and she blinked rapidly before any tears could escape. "Thank you." Her voice nearly broke as she said the words.

Oh goodness. Air. She needed air.

Madison strode through the back door and onto the peeling wraparound porch. The breeze coming off the ocean attacked Madison's hair. From here, the wooden boardwalk that spanned the length of the town was only a stone's throw away. It wound like a slatted snake across the sparkling sands, where the Pacific whooshed in and out. Even on this Monday in early January, a handful of tourists and villagers walked the beach, enjoying the quiet landscape that was so different from the big cities of Los Angeles and San Francisco. Walker Beach was a few hundred miles from each and a world unto itself.

She may not have missed Walker Beach—or most of its people—but nothing could compete with this view.

"Hey."

Madison jumped and spun at the intrusion, fixing what she hoped was an intimidating glare on Evan, who now leaned against the doorjamb, hands tucked inside his pockets.

"I was just kidding about the five-months thing. I didn't mind helping out. I'm sure you've had a lot going on with school."

"How did you know about that?" She'd only just graduated three weeks ago, and life since then had been a whirlwind of packing her apartment and celebrating the holidays with her grandma in San Francisco.

"Chrissy told me." Evan shrugged. "She made it sound like you wouldn't want to keep the business or the house but knew it may help you out financially to sell them. I actually wasn't sure if you'd come yourself or just send movers to pack up everything."

Madison had considered it, but someone had to do Chrissy's things justice. Grandma hadn't wanted anything to do with Walker Beach since Grandpa had died. She hadn't even held Chrissy's funeral here.

So it was up to Madison, who had received the shock of her life when she'd been named heir of Chrissy's house and the hardware store that had been in the family for fifty years. It had taken her some time to work up her courage, but she was here now, with the perfect window of time before her dream job began. She'd get Chrissy's things sorted, her store inventoried, and her house and Hole-in-the-Wall Hardware on the market. Easy peasy.

But wait. Evan acted like . . . "So, you knew she was sick?" It wasn't something her aunt had shared with anyone in her family, including Madison. But perhaps she'd known that Madison would have abandoned her last year of school in a heartbeat if the word *cancer* had crossed her lips. It was the least she would have done for the woman who had taken in her twelve-year-old niece when Madison had lost her parents in a freak avalanche during a ski trip in Vermont.

Evan kicked at a rock on the patio. "Yeah."

"She didn't tell me." Madison swallowed hard. She should have been there. She should have known. If she'd bothered to come back to Walker Beach . . . But the town had held such painful memories—or so she'd told herself. Aunt Chrissy had come several times to visit Madison in Los Angeles, and Madison had counted that as enough.

But she'd left her aunt alone when she'd needed Madison most.

"I'm sorry."

Well, not completely alone. Apparently, Evan Walsh had been there.

Madison studied him, but no matter how hard she looked, he was an enigma. The expression in his eyes was clearly pained, but her pain and anger wouldn't let her embrace his. Chrissy had been Madison's aunt, and this was Madison's store. She didn't need Evan's help anymore.

She squared her shoulders. "I appreciate you keeping an eye on things, but I'm here now."

He nodded, quietly accepting her words, which had come out a bit harsher than she'd intended. "How long will you be here?" His question sounded nervous, though she couldn't imagine why it should.

"I'm not sure. There's a lot to do."

"Let me know if you need any help."

Help? From him? She'd sooner swim in the freezing-cold ocean and take a subsequent dip in a vat of ice. But she'd never let him know how much he'd wounded her in the past. It didn't matter anymore. She was over it, and she was better for it.

Madison jutted her chin forward. "I don't think I will, but thanks."

He eyed her for a moment. "Guess I'll go, then." Turning, he started down the cracked steps.

"Wait. Evan?"

"Yeah?" He circled back, and something in his eyes looked hopeful. But that was silly.

"I'll take your key."

"Oh. Right." Pulling the key from his pocket, his fingers brushed her palm as he handed it to her.

"Thanks." Madison rubbed away the fire that fanned from the spot where he'd touched her to the tips of her fingers.

They stared at each other until the ringing of her phone shattered the silence between them.

Madison pulled the phone from her back pocket, swiveled on her heel, and marched inside the store. She closed the back door in such haste that it slammed.

Why had she let the man rattle her so much? Or maybe it was simply being back here, in a place she couldn't help but love because of its previous owner. Yes, that had to be it. Evan Walsh was nothing to her. She needed to remember that.

The phone continued to blare. Oh, right. Without looking at the Caller ID, Madison clicked the green button on her screen. "Hello?"

"Is this Madison?"

"Yes. Who is this?" Madison slid into the nearest chair at the two-person table in the break room.

"Courtney Lambdon at Lola Public Library."

Her future boss. "Hi. How are you?"

"Not so great, actually. I hate to be the bearer of bad news, but the grant money we were planning to use to fund your position fell through. I'm afraid we can no longer offer you the job."

"What?" This had to be a sick joke. She'd already sublet her apartment in L.A., quit her job at the bookstore, packed. "There's nothing you can do?"

"I'm sorry, but no. We will, of course, search for other grant opportunities, but there is no guarantee we'll get one. If we do, I will let you know as soon as possible."

That wasn't good enough. She needed a job now. Maybe she could reach out to other libraries. She'd prefer to stay on the West Coast, but it didn't matter where, really. It wasn't like she had any real roots tying her down.

But that would take time and a bit of luck. She'd been lucky to find the job in Oregon.

Madison issued a weak thank you to Courtney and hung up the phone. Groaning, she rubbed her temples. What was she going to do now?

Her eyes caught sight of a sign hanging over the doorway: Follow Your Dreams. How many times had Aunt Chrissy told her that?

"Yeah, I tried, Aunt Chrissy. And look where it got me."

Back in the last place she wanted to be with nothing but a house and a store she'd never asked for.

The meeting had to go off without a hitch if Evan was going to snag this deal for Walker Beach.

And, simultaneously, a win for his dad.

And possibly a promotion.

Yeah, there was definitely a lot riding on the next hour of his life.

"You ready, son?"

Evan glanced up to find Jim Walsh in the doorway of the tiny office inside City Hall that Evan shared with two other workers.

"Be right there." Evan closed Excel and locked his computer before standing then snatched the stack of spiral-bound proposals from the edge of his desk.

"Good luck," Alex Rosche, a financial analyst for the city, said as Evan passed.

Their other office mate—his boss, Denise—was currently out on maternity leave, though rumor had it she wouldn't be coming back. If it were true, of course he'd miss her, but that left her job wide-open for the taking, so long as the board didn't go with an outside hire.

Evan would just have to continue to prove his worth.

"Thanks, man." As he stepped outside the office into the hallway, Evan's dress shoes squeaked on the polished floor. In this moment, he'd give anything to be in a T-shirt and shorts, running bases and hitting balls in the glorious outdoors.

But he'd messed up that dream a long time ago. No sense in longing for something that was in the past. Time to focus on what was ahead, on what could elevate him in the eyes of all the townspeople—including dear old Dad—who still saw the lazy screw-up he'd been. The one who'd thrown away a baseball scholarship for a night of drinking with his buddies.

His father glanced up from his phone then shoved it into the clip on his belt. He eyed the proposals in Evan's arms. "I don't need to remind you what's at stake here."

"I know, Dad."

"Good."

At fifty-one, Jim Walsh cut an imposing six-foot figure, with broad shoulders and a full head of black hair that he had never colored to Evan's knowledge. From the time Evan was young, his father had been a successful businessman, and almost four years ago, he'd won his first bid as mayor. But elections were coming up later this year, so despite all the good he'd accomplished, it was important for him to continue garnering wins to keep his service fresh in Walker Beach residents' minds.

Herman Hardware would be just such a win—a large one—with the potential to lower costs for those in need of home improvement tools and services and to increase the number of jobs in town.

And that's where Evan came in. As the town's assistant community development officer, he worked with his boss to secure grants from various sources and determine where to disperse the funds. But an even bigger part of his job was the focus on revitalizing Walker Beach's downtown, which included attracting new businesses to the area as well as helping those already there stay afloat.

He and his father started down the hall together, passing other city officials who called out greetings to Evan and Mayor Walsh.

"Evan, Mayor." Jack Campbell leaned heavily on his cane and extended his right hand. Every month the man's stage 4 kidney failure became more apparent, leaving him with a yellow pallor and a thinning hairline, though the latter wasn't unusual for a man in his late fifties.

"How are you, Jack?" Evan shook the man's hand.

His dad did the same, though Evan didn't miss the quick glance he gave his watch.

Jack shuddered in a breath, but peace radiated in his eyes. "I'm good, I'm good. Looking forward to having Derek home from France in a few months. He's going to help me put that grant money to good use."

"That's awesome. I can't wait to see him again."

"Me too, me too." Jack cleared his throat. "I can't thank you enough for securing that money for us. I don't know what I would have done if we'd lost the vineyard."

"I'm only sorry it wasn't more." What he'd been able to

secure for the Campbells would only see Jack through the next harvest. It wasn't enough—it never was—but Evan had done what he could for his buddy's family.

"Nonsense. That money gives us the chance to bring new life to the business. I'm hoping to implement several new processes and hire even more workers for the harvest this year. You're doing good work. Jim, you should be proud of this one."

Evan probably looked like a kid who'd aced his first spelling test, but he couldn't hold back his grin. "Thank you, sir."

His dad slapped Evan on the back. "He's just doing his job."

Yep, there came the inevitable pricking of his inflated spirit. "Right, of course. I'm happy to help the community." And he really was. But it was nice to see his long days sometimes impacted people's lives.

Tilting his head, Jack squinted. "I heard a rumor that the hardware store may be opening again?" He winked. "If so, you're on a roll. That sure would be a nice boon to our town. People are tired of driving all the way to San Luis to buy a hammer and some paint. I know there's online shopping, but there's nothing quite like browsing an actual store."

Dad jumped in. "Your council members, including myself, are well-aware of this problem, and we are working to get it solved. Don't you worry."

"I'm not worried. Not with Evan here at the helm." Jack waved them off. "I'm sure you were on your way somewhere important, so I won't keep you. Just wanted to say thanks." He turned and headed toward the heavy oak front door.

"We're late, son. Let's go." Dad started back toward the conference room.

"Be right there." Evan crossed the hallway to the door before Jack could reach it. "Allow me." He opened the door for the man, who squeezed his arm in thanks as he passed.

Once he'd left, Evan let go of the door and caught up with Dad.

Dad grunted. "That was smart, actually. He might be sick as a dog, but Campbell is an influential member of the fifty-five and older crowd. Good work, son."

Did it always have to devolve into politics with him? "That's not . . ." Gripping the stack of proposals, Evan frowned. "The door is heavy. It would have been hard for him to open on his own."

"Of course, of course."

Evan and his dad arrived at the conference room, where a twelve-person table and its accompanying chairs took up nearly the entire space. Most of the seats were already occupied by a mix of people—some from the city council, some from Herman Hardware. As planned, his dad's assistant, Greta, had already seated their guests and provided them with water and coffee.

Chatter stopped, and everyone looked expectantly at them. Before Evan could greet them, his dad spoke. "Sorry we're late. Evan here was putting the final touches on everything. But thank you all for coming." He shook hands all around and slid into a seat at the head of the table, leaving the one next to it open for Evan.

"Yes, thank you for being here, everyone." He made eye contact with each person from Herman Hardware, including a short man with a wide girth—Hank Aldrin, the guy they really needed to impress—and Roxy Chamberlain, Aldrin's assistant and Evan's ex-girlfriend from high school. Now she lived in San Fran, working in the headquarters for Herman, a regional hardware chain with great reach and a small-town feel perfect for Walker Beach.

Despite his and Roxy's long-ago breakup, they were still on decent speaking terms. In fact, she was the one who'd told Evan that Herman was looking to open a handful of new locations in California.

Evan passed out the proposals then sat next to Dad. "I hope the drive down wasn't too bad today."

Mr. Aldrin pulled a pair of readers from his jacket pocket and slid them on. "Not too bad, no, though we had to leave so early that I didn't get my breakfast." He picked up the proposal and began to peruse it. If only the man weren't so difficult to read. Roxy had warned Evan that Aldrin, the company's vice president of regional development, liked to be incredibly thorough, so Evan had spent the last week agonizing over this proposal.

Evan turned to Greta, who sat on the other side of Dad, pen poised over a notebook. "Greta, since our guests haven't had a chance to eat, would you mind making a trip to the Frosted Cake? I'll reimburse you later."

Greta nodded and stood. "Of course." She hurried from the room.

Mr. Aldrin's eyebrow rose. "The Frosted Cake?"

Evan leaned back in his chair. "When you need a donut fix, there's nothing better. Trust me on this one. They're heaven."

Aldrin grunted. "Hope that doesn't mean I'll die of a heart attack when I eat one." But the corner of his large lips lifted, and Evan mentally whooped when the crowd broke out in a round of chuckles.

The tension effectively broken, Evan tugged on the cuffs of his suit jacket. "While we're waiting for our late morning snack to arrive, should we get into the proposal?"

After a moment of nods and murmurs of agreement, he continued. "Since our initial conversation, I've put together this proposal with the advantages to your company and our town." He rattled off a list of facts. "In short, I believe Walker Beach and Herman would serve each other well."

From the corner of his eye, he caught his father's nod of approval.

Evan hoped he could bring this home.

Mr. Aldrin adjusted his glasses and looked up. "One of the major concerns I have is the lagging economy due to the earthquake that occurred six months ago. I realize I've only taken a cursory glance at this, but do you address that at all? Have your businesses seen a decrease in revenue since then?"

"Yes, if you turn to page six"—the room filled with the sound of rustling paper—"you'll see our plan for continuing to revive the economy. I'm not going to pretend that the earthquake had no effect."

The small California city's downtown was unofficially divided into the more historic South Village and the more modern North Village, and the whole town sat just west of Pacific Highway 1. Rolling hills on the east side of town boasted tall green trees, some of which had fallen in the earthquake, devastating several homes in the region. "At least fifty residences and ten local businesses in our North Village were damaged, including a prominent inn along the beach. Our public library was also damaged and has yet to reopen."

Brow crinkled, Mr. Aldrin looked as if he were about to ask more, so Evan rushed to finish his thought. "Tourism has been affected slightly, but as soon as more businesses get back on their feet, the better. We've been able to secure extra grant money we hope to use to help our local businesses succeed. And as I mentioned earlier, we offer fabulous tax incentives for new businesses coming in."

"Not only that, but this is the year Walker Beach will celebrate one hundred and fifty years since its inception." Evan's father leaned forward, an excited glint in his eyes. "We are planning a sesquicentennial celebration in December, and it is bound to attract hordes of tourists from miles around."

"Thanks, Mayor Walsh." Evan turned back to Mr. Aldrin and team. "What other questions do you have? We want nothing more than to ease your mind about this entire process."

"As you know, Mr. Herman insists that each of our small-town locations is integrated into the downtown. Do you have the space for that?"

"Yes, in fact, right now we have the perfect location in mind."

The two storefronts next to Hole-in-the-Wall Hardware had been available for some time and would suit Herman Hardware well. Of course, Evan never would have considered it—or invited Herman Hardware to move in at all—if Chrissy had still been here.

Although her niece was. But just temporarily.

Meeting Madison Price yesterday . . . wow. There was something about the curl of her brown hair, her piercing eyes, the hug of her jeans against her hips that had made him feel like a preteen with his first crush. But it wasn't just her beauty. The woman Chrissy had described was quiet and shy, but Madison had held herself with confidence, unafraid to look him in the eye.

He hadn't felt an attraction like that toward someone in a long time.

Evan tugged at his collar. At the sudden quiet in the room, he glanced up. Everyone—including Dad with his narrowed eyes—was staring at him. Uh-oh. He'd missed something. Great. If he wanted the job of head community developer, he'd need to remain much more focused. "I'm sorry, can you repeat that, please?"

Mr. Aldrin's frown deepened, and beside him, Roxy's lips twitched.

"Mr. Aldrin was just asking about the hardware store that's currently in town." The heat of Dad's glare simmered onto Evan's skin. "But that's not a problem, is it?"

Had someone turned up the heat in here? A dip in the ocean sounded refreshing right about now. "I don't believe so, no."

Dad's fake smile wavered. Okay, definitely not the right thing to say.

Evan tried again. "That is, the former owner passed away almost five months ago, and the new owner has just arrived back in town. As far as I know, she doesn't have plans to reopen it." Madison had said so.

At least, he thought she had. Maybe he'd just assumed.

"Of course, we'll confirm that right away. It shouldn't be a problem." Dad quirked an eyebrow at Evan.

"Right. No problem at all." From what Chrissy had told him, Madison would never stay and run the store. But he didn't know for sure what she was planning. Still, with the way Dad and Mr. Aldrin were looking at him, he needed to make some sort of assurances so this deal didn't die a sudden, horrible death.

"I'll be frank." Mr. Aldrin removed his glasses. "Walker Beach is not the only location we are considering. If there is already a viable competitor here, that will make this town a no-go for us. That combined with the earthquake aftermath and the incentives that other locations are offering . . . well, I'll confer with Mr. Herman, but at this point, I'm just not sure we are going to be able to make this work."

No, no, no. This was all going downhill so quickly. "Of course you're entitled to your opinion, but I believe Walker Beach is the best town there is." If it weren't, Evan would have been on a plane to anywhere else a long time ago. "The people here are resilient. We have heart, sir, and that's not something you can say about every other town. What can we do to turn this around for you?"

Much as he tried, Evan couldn't keep the pleading out of his tone. Sure, in isolation, this deal wouldn't make or break his bid for Denise's job. But like Jack had said, people had been clamoring for a hardware store option ever since Chrissy had closed-up shop. If he succeeded, people would love him for it. If he failed, he was one step further away from everything he wanted. He'd have to work that much harder to prove himself.

Mr. Aldrin shut the proposal booklet and stood. "I'm not sure there is anything you can do."

It didn't matter how hard he'd worked. Evan had indeed failed.

Again.

And the look on Dad's face said he'd never really expected any differently.

CHAPTER 2

Had her aunt ever heard of a file cabinet?

Madison groaned as she sifted through the piles of papers on Aunt Chrissy's desk, ensconced in the tiny office at the back of the store. How she'd managed to keep the store afloat all these years with her level of disorganization was a wonder.

And all by herself too.

How had she done it, day in and day out, bearing the load alone? Not to mention the quiet of this place, which was enough to drive Madison batty. Even though libraries were zones of quiet, they had energy, one that pulsed and hummed with life thanks to the thousands of stories surrounding their patrons.

A light rain plinked against the window as Madison tried to make sense of her aunt's system of organization—assuming she had one. The papers in front of her seemed to be bills, but whether they'd been paid or not was anyone's guess. And then, toward the edge . . . were those invoices? And good, there was the lease agreement. She made a mental note to look at that later since she'd need to inform the landlord that she intended to sell the business.

At least the ledger seemed to be in decent condition, although it would have been nice if her aunt had finally embraced the miracle of digital accounting.

Her head pounded, whether from being in a room lit only by a single lamp in the corner and the gray daylight that managed to filter through the clouds or just from the pure exhaustion, she couldn't tell. Being among Aunt Chrissy's things during the last few days had left Madison with an aching heart and an inability to sleep.

As did the fact she was currently jobless with no prospects on the horizon.

Madison picked up the top paper in a new pile she had yet to examine. It seemed to be a printed email, so perhaps this stack was personal correspondence? As she set the page back down, a name popped out at her. Evan Walsh. Her eyes quickly skimmed the contents of the paper. Evan's email signature identified him as Walker Beach's assistant community development officer, and the message string was about some board Aunt Chrissy had been on. Purely business, nothing personal about it.

Yet, what had Evan said the other day? Something about how he and Aunt Chrissy had gotten close before she died. How had that come to be? Madison hadn't seen Evan since their encounter on her first day back to town, and most of her was OK with that. But some part also wanted to ask him to elaborate, to tell her about Aunt Chrissy's last days.

Ugh. She needed a break.

Madison fled the dank room and walked to the front of the store where she'd left her book this morning. Flicking on the wall switch, she flooded the place with light. Once again, the sight in front of her stole her ability to breathe.

It was as if she'd stepped into a time machine. Nothing had changed during the last decade. Oh sure, the supplies were more modern, and the walls had received a fresh coat of bright yellow paint. But the display of colorful paint cans glued to the white brick wall, the collection of quirky shovels and tools hanging from the ceiling above the front window, the always-present Christmas tree in the corner—those things had Madison just waiting for Chrissy to walk in from the back, crack her knuckles, and say, "Here's to another great day!"

A tear pushed through her defenses and slipped down her cheek. Man, she missed her aunt. Staying away from here, she'd been able to convince herself that Aunt Chrissy wasn't really gone. But now there was no denying it, even though her aunt's palpable presence permeated every square inch of this place.

Her book. She needed to read, to escape. Madison located her purse sitting on the front desk and rummaged inside. But instead of her novel, she pulled out the letter she'd received just that morning—mail forwarding had worked much more quickly than she'd anticipated—and slumped against the wall.

When she'd missed the deadline to apply for federal aid at her university the first time, she'd taken out a private loan with a small credit union in Los Angeles, and the interest rate had been outrageous. She'd been stupid, but school had been so important to her. Unfortunately, while they'd allowed her to defer payments until graduation, they didn't offer any grace periods afterward, which meant her first payment was due next month. It wasn't necessarily for an outrageous amount of money, but it was still more than she had in her bank account.

All the money Aunt Chrissy had left her had been used to pay the mortgage on her properties and for Madison's last semester of school. Selling the store and house wouldn't bring in any money until the sales were final—and who knew how quickly they'd even sell?—but she needed money pronto.

A knock on the door interrupted her desperate thoughts. Madison stuffed the letter back into her purse and glanced up. Someone in an orange jacket huddled just outside.

Madison walked over and cracked the door to find a thirty-something man clutching a toddler's hand. "Sorry, we aren't open."

The street and sidewalks behind the pair were wet, and gray clouds rolled gently across the horizon.

"I saw your light on and hoped . . ." The guy hugged his daughter close to his leg. "Our car broke down out front, and I don't have any battery cables. I thought if I could buy some, surely someone would stop and give me a jump."

"I'd love to help, b—"

"It's my wife's birthday, and Lucy and I were picking up a piece of artwork from next door—we're not from around here, just visiting—and of course the car wouldn't start after we got back in. But my wife has had a rough few months, and we just need to get her this present . . ." The guy's eyes pleaded with Madison. His little girl's lip trembled.

Madison sighed. "I don't know if we have what you need, but you're welcome to see." She widened the door opening, and the man ushered his daughter inside. "I'm afraid I don't know where they'd be."

She didn't know where anything would be. Who was she kidding? She didn't even know what half the items in this store were.

"No worries. I'll just have a look around if you don't mind."

"Be my guest."

While the man perused, Madison tidied up the desk. A few minutes later, he and his daughter approached, a triumphant look in his eye and a package of red rope-looking things with handles in his hand. "Found them! What do I owe you?"

"Oh, uh. You can just have them."

"No way. The least I can do is pay for them."

Madison bit her lip. "What do you think is fair?"

The man shrugged. "I don't know. Twenty bucks?"

"Sold." She opened the drawer of the desk, tugged a note off the sticky pad, and wrote a "receipt" for him. "Oh, wait, I don't have a way to take a credit card."

"I've got cash." He pulled a twenty from his wallet and held it out to her. "Thank you so much again. You saved us." Then he left the same way he'd come.

Huh. That was . . . interesting.

Madison picked up her book again, losing herself for several minutes in another world.

The bell jangled over the door. She'd forgotten to lock it. "Sorry, we are—"

"Holy cow! Madison, is that you?" A willowy blonde pulled a wireless headphone from her right ear. Dressed in hot-pink pants and a sleek black jogging jacket, her long hair strung up in a messy ponytail, she looked like she belonged on the cover of *Runner's World*.

"Ashley?"

"It *is* you!" Ashley Baker shot forward, and they embraced. "How are you? I can't believe it's you. Girl, you look amazing!"

"Thanks." Madison pushed her hair behind her ear. "I'm good. What about you? You look great as well."

"Aw, you're sweet. When did you get back into town, anyway? Normally I'd have heard something from the Walker Beach gossips." A silly grin slid across her face.

That made Madison laugh as well, which felt good after the way she'd been feeling the last few days. Of course, Ash had always been good at bringing Madison out of her shell, being just about the only friend Madison had here. They'd drifted apart a bit in high school due to the natural course of things—Ashley being as involved in sports and other clubs as she was, Madison being the loner *she* was.

But the woman acted as if they hadn't missed a beat. And maybe, in her mind, they truly hadn't.

Warmth stirred inside Madison's chest. "My aunt left the store and her house to me, so I'm here to prep them for sale."

That sobered Ashley right up. "I'm so sorry about Chrissy. We all miss her. She was such a light in this town."

"Thanks." Madison bit her lip. "What are you up to these days?"

Ashley tugged her ponytail around and played with the ends. "Oh, a little of this, a little of that. I work for a company in town as an events coordinator. Weddings, bar mitzvahs, corporate retreats, that sort of thing. It's fun. I run and hike in my free time. Not that there's much of that." She cocked her head. "So, you're only here for a little bit?"

As Madison opened her mouth to reply, a sixty-something Hispanic couple breezed in through the front door. Goodness, she let one guy in and the whole town thought it was a free-for-all. "We aren't—"

"Open, we know." The man, who wore a sheriff's star pinned to his green law enforcement uniform, had the decency to give a sheepish grin. "You're Chrissy Price's girl, aren't you?"

"Her niece, yes."

"I'm Sheriff Rodriguez. You going to be in town long?"

"Well . . ."

His wife swatted his arm. "Don't be so nosy, José. You're off duty as of ten minutes ago." She returned her attention to Madison. "I promise we didn't come here to interrogate you. We just helped jump-start the car for a sweet man and his daughter, and he said you let him buy some cables. We've been in desperate need of a plunger and haven't had a chance to drive to the nearest store. Would it be a terrible inconvenience if we just . . ."

Inwardly sighing, Madison gestured toward the first aisle. "Sure. Go ahead."

"Thanks, young lady." The sheriff tipped his hat to her and disappeared around the corner with his wife.

Ashley leaned against the counter. "You sure you want to sell? People around here have been itching for a new hardware store. You'd have built-in business."

"I don't know anything about running a hardware store. Besides, I just finished my master's in library science. I had a job in Oregon lined up, but the funding fell through. So I'm just here until I figure out what to do next."

"That must have been disappointing." Ashley's face lit up, and she snapped her fingers. "We may have a librarian job opening here sometime soon. It also depends on funding, though, and it could be months before we get it approved, if we even do."

Too bad it wasn't a for sure thing—though, from now on, Madison was going to have a hard time trusting any job that relied on grant money. And besides, a library job in Walker Beach would mean she'd have to stay . . . in Walker Beach. No thanks. Too many bad memories.

She cleared her throat. "What happened to Mrs. Wildman?" The volunteer librarian had been Madison's first boss when she'd worked as a library aide in high school. Though she hadn't been paid in money, she'd gotten the first pick of all the old books being cast-off to make room for new ones. She'd felt like she'd won the lottery every time.

"She's ready to retire. I guess she's been wanting to for a while, and she's gotten a taste of what that would be like over the last six months."

"Why is that?"

"The library has been closed."

"Closed?"

"Sorry to interrupt. I'm ready to check out, dear." The sheriff's wife shuffled forward with a plunger and a power tool of some kind while the sheriff took a call outside. "He saw the drill and remembered our son wants one for his birthday. I hope you don't mind."

"Oh, OK. Sure." They were doing her a favor, really. Fewer things to inventory, right?

The woman paid her suggested price—which she'd pulled

out of thin air—and walked out, only to be met by a few other townspeople who entered. Madison didn't even bother telling them she wasn't open.

She turned back to Ashley, whose lips were tugged in a smile.

"Seems like you're doing fine for someone who doesn't know anything about running a hardware store."

Madison rolled her eyes. "So, what were you saying about the library?"

"The earthquake last year nearly destroyed the building and lots of its contents."

Chrissy had told her about the earthquake. She'd only experienced a small bit of damage to her store, with things rattling and falling off the walls. Other shops hadn't been so lucky.

"The library flooded as a result. We were renting a space from a local realtor, and it turns out the renter's insurance policy we had wasn't great. Bare minimum, in fact." Ashley tapped her earbud against the desktop. "And we haven't been able to reopen."

A town without a library. What a shame. "Why not?"

"Several reasons. All the insurance stuff took forever to come through, and we need a new location, which has been hard to find. Hey, if you have any time while you're here, I could use your opinion on books that would be great to order for our new collection." When Madison shot her a confused look, Ashley rushed on. "I'm actually one of the newest members of the Walker Beach library board. The town was hard-up for committee members, so I volunteered. The rest of the board is older, and their tastes aren't exactly in line with those of the younger generations. And I'm not a huge reader, so I'm a bit lost on what to get."

"Sure, I'm happy to point you in the right direction if I have time."

"Great." Ashley pulled her phone from her jacket pocket and

clicked it on. “Oh man, I’ve gotta run. I’m meeting my brother Ben’s girlfriend and my cousin Shannon for dinner. Do you remember Shannon? She’s a year younger than us.”

“Vaguely.” The Bakers were one of the biggest families here in Walker Beach—the kind with a few landmarks named after them—and it was hard to keep track of them all. “It was good to see you.”

“Do you want to come with us? I’m sure Shannon and Bella won’t mind. And I’d love to hear more about what’s going on in your life.”

The eagerness on Ashley’s face made Madison almost want to say yes. Almost.

“That sounds fun, but I have so much work to do here.” And she still had a shop full of people—maybe about ten had entered in the few minutes that she and Ashley had been talking. “Maybe another time?”

“Of course.” Ashley paused, touching Madison’s arm. “I can keep you posted on the librarian job. If by some miracle you stayed, you’d make me the happiest woman in the world. Too many people I care about have left.” She flashed Madison a sad smile before heading out the door.

Yeah, Madison wasn’t holding her breath. Even if she had a desire to stay here, the library job sounded like it was months off. And the bills in Madison’s purse were a stark reminder that she needed money now.

Madison thrust on a smile as a customer approached. And then another. And another.

Finally, after the last straggler left, the clock read eight. Madison’s eyelids were heavy, and she leaned against the desk, rubbing her temples. There was no way she was going to have the energy to do any more work on the store tonight. Sure, she might have sold a few items, but she’d just lost an afternoon of good work hours that she could have spent cleaning and organizing.

It had been amazing how one person after another trickled in. She hadn't done a thing except stand there and take people's money. Must have been the easiest couple hundred she'd ever made.

Curious, she reached for the stack of bills she'd shoved into a Kleenex box she'd found under the desk. As she counted, her eyes widened and her heart sped up.

She recounted.

No way. That wasn't possible.

In the course of four hours, on a rainy Wednesday afternoon and evening, she'd made $903. Her first school loan repayment had just been covered. Almost her second one too.

What if . . .

No. She couldn't stay. Not here.

And yet, she needed a job. A house.

She already had both. Here.

No, not a dream job, but one that would be steady and secure. Aunt Chrissy had never mentioned financial troubles, and Ashley had said the townspeople really wanted a hardware store again. Hole-in-the-Wall Hardware could be the answer to their collective needs.

Yeah, she didn't know anything about running a business—and a hardware store in particular—but she was smart. She could learn.

And yes, she'd have to get over that the job happened to be in Walker Beach. But she could do that. Madison wasn't the same girl who had walked the halls of Walker Beach High School, crying anytime someone whispered "Lizard Lady" in her ear. She was strong, and she knew her worth.

And people who were strong took decisive actions. They didn't wait for others to rescue them. No one was going to rescue Madison—no one, maybe, except for Aunt Chrissy, who'd left her this opportunity in the first place.

That was it. She was doing it.

Hole-in-the-Wall Hardware was going to open for business once again.

~

After a full day of budget meetings that had kept Evan locked in a conference room with his father, only one thing would put a smile back on his face—a meal from the Frosted Cake.

Specifically, their meatloaf and mashed potatoes. Yeah, those babies were gonna get him through another long night at the dark and lonely office.

But that beat going home to an even lonelier apartment, with only his cat Jeter for company.

"Here ya go, sugar." From behind the pastry display case, Josephine Radcliffe handed Evan a paper bag with The Frosted Cake stamped on the front. As usual, the brightly lit bakery-slash-restaurant bustled with Walker Beach residents just off work and looking for a good meal and friendly company.

From its tables in back with floral tablecloths to racks of spices and jams for sale in the corner and a huge painting of a pink VW Bug hanging on the far wall, this café was Walker Beach through and through—as was its white-haired owner with the ready smile and ample hugs.

"You know the way to a man's heart." He unrolled the top of the bag and breathed in the scent of homestyle cooking Ms. Josephine was famous for. She'd even added an extra roll—and all Walker Beach regulars knew her bread was worth its weight in gold. "If you weren't married, I'd propose to you right now. Tell Arnie I say hello, by the way."

"I will. He's enjoying the retired life while I slave away." The sixty-something grandma winked at him and wagged her finger. "And you save that proposal for some young lady who will surely appreciate it. You got anyone special yet?"

Evan closed the bag and laughed. "I'm married to my job right now."

"Well, you're doing a mighty fine job reviving the downtown. I heard the hardware store is back open for business."

He frowned. Somehow, the news about Herman Hardware must have leaked out—but obviously not the whole story. "I don't think that's happening anymore."

"What do you mean? Hilda told me just this morning that she and José were in there last night shopping."

"In where?"

"Now, sugar, you must be tired. I just told you. The hardware store."

"As in, Hole-in-the-Wall Hardware?"

"What other hardware store do you know of in town?" Josephine laughed. "Well, speak of the angel herself. Madison Price, I hear you're back for the long haul."

Evan turned. "Madison." Seriously? Why had his voice chosen that instant to sound like a prepubescent teen? He cleared this throat. "Hey."

Somehow, despite her yoga pants and wrinkled shirt, she looked even more beautiful today than she had earlier this week in skinny jeans and a fitted sweater.

Ignoring him, she maneuvered past and approached the counter, where Ms. Josephine had a to-go bag waiting. "Hey, Ms. Josephine." She smiled, the effect mesmerizing his focus. "It's great to see you again. And you heard right."

She had? Evan scrubbed a hand across his face as he waited for Madison to pay for her food.

Madison turned around, bag in hand. Surprise lit her features when she saw him still standing there but was soon replaced with something like annoyance—brows raised, nose scrunched, lips curled. Even that didn't diminish her beauty or the vulnerability floating just beneath the surface.

Had he done something to offend her? Maybe she'd heard

somehow about Herman Hardware. Things didn't stay quiet in this town for long. Not that she had anything to worry about. Mr. Aldrin had looked pretty settled in his opinion when he'd left the meeting yesterday, and Evan hadn't heard a word from anyone at Herman since.

"So, what's this about you reopening the hardware store?"

Maybe she didn't want him to notice the way she bit her lip, inhaling twice in rapid succession, but he did. "I haven't officially reopened yet. I was just in there yesterday and people kept coming in. So I let them." With a whirl, she hightailed it out of the café's front door.

"Hang on." He followed and caught up with her in front of Charmed, I'm Sure Books. "What you said to Ms. Josephine, though . . . that made it sound like you were planning to stick around."

Madison continued her brisk pace without looking at him. She clutched the Frosted Cake bag in her fist. "So what if I am?"

The sidewalk was always pretty crowded this time of day and today was no exception. As Madison bulldozed her way past people ducking into various South Village shops and restaurants—from Hardings Market to Froggies Pizza and Rodolfo's Taqueria—Evan did his best to keep up.

Finally, he snagged her elbow. She stopped abruptly, her eyes darting to his fingers. He let go immediately. "Sorry, it's just kind of hard to talk while walking so fast."

"I have a lot of work to do at the store. And we really don't have anything to talk about."

"Actually, there was something I'd like to discuss, if you don't mind." He tilted his head, smiling. "Can we go beachside? May as well enjoy the walk and get some extra breathing room in the meantime."

Her teeth snagged her bottom lip, and he couldn't help staring for a moment. "I guess." Then she turned down an alley that led out to the sand, and Evan once again followed her. She stopped at the boardwalk and waited for him to catch up. Her shoulders straightened. "What did you want to talk about?"

The waning sun from the day backlit Madison, silhouetting her slim figure. They started walking, together this time, along the wide boardwalk. Occasional cyclists and kids on rollerblades passed, but for the most part, they were alone. The ocean to their right filled in the silence as he considered the best way to approach the topic.

"So, are you?"

"Am I what?"

"Planning to reopen the store."

"Why do you care?"

Evan nearly stumbled at the clenched tone. Wow. Had Madison always been this prickly? Chrissy had described her as sweet, shy, and studious. He glanced at her and caught her wince.

"Sorry, that was rude. I'm going on only a few hours of sleep, but that's no excuse."

"It's OK. I get it." His gaze found hers. "And I care for a couple of reasons, one being Chrissy. She was a true friend to me when I didn't have many, so I care what happens to her store."

He shoved his free hand into the pocket of his slacks, an empty feeling gnawing at his chest. Chrissy Price had been the first one to believe in him—the only one, really. He'd come into her shop to buy a new wrench three years ago, and she'd asked if he'd mind helping her with a plumbing issue her landlord hadn't had time to fix. Afterward, she'd served him lemonade and some killer chocolate chip cookies, and they'd sat on her back porch chatting about life.

That had become their weekly routine. He'd stop by and help her with something around the shop, and she'd dish up some sweets and wisdom.

It was because of her encouragement, her belief in a screw-up like him, that he'd finally gotten his life on track—away from the alcohol, the parties, the recreational drugs and on toward something meaningful.

The sun slipped past the horizon and tall lamps along the boardwalk popped on, dousing him and Madison in artificial light.

Their pace slowed. Madison seemed to be thinking, her face contorted. Finally, she spoke. "Yeah, I've decided to stay. To reopen the store."

Oh, wow. "What made you decide to do that?"

A shrug. "The library job I had lined up fell through, and people clearly want a hardware store in town. Seemed like the logical thing to do."

She didn't appear to have the same passion for the store that Chrissy had, but Madison seemed smart enough. Given the several generations of Prices to own Hole-in-the-Wall Hardware, running the store was in her blood.

And the people *did* want a hardware store. He'd thought Herman was the answer. But maybe . . .

He cleared his throat. "That's great. So, what's the plan? What do you still need to do before you can open?"

"Unfortunately, I don't know the first thing about running a business, so I'm not sure. I've been trying to organize Aunt Chrissy's records, but that's driving me up a wall."

"She wasn't the neatest of people, was she?"

"No. There's a huge storeroom filled with boxes, and I don't have any clue what's in them yet. I'm a little afraid to find out. I guess I could just go ahead and reopen the store and see what happens, but the research librarian in me is apprehensive to dive in like that."

And here was his opening. His chance to snag a win for the community despite not winning the contract with Herman. And if he could be Madison's hero in the meantime, well . . . "I could help."

"Help? How?"

"I work with businesses all the time to come up with plans to help them stand out, which includes doing a deep dive into their assets and liabilities." He pushed past the tension and flexed with his free arm. "And I've been told I'm rather strong. I can help move boxes with the best of them."

How he wanted Madison to crack a grin along with him, but she remained as stoic as ever. Evan racked his brain, trying to think of something he'd done to make her so guarded around him. But he hadn't known her back when she'd lived here, and their two interactions this week hadn't been enough to cause this kind of reaction—at least, he didn't think so. Maybe she was just like this with everyone.

Before he could gather the courage to ask her if he'd done something offensive, they reached the back porch of Hole-in-the-Wall Hardware.

Madison turned, pulling the brown paper bag to her chest. "Thanks for the offer." Pools of uncertainty flooded her eyes, and she fiddled with a strand of hair. Evan had the strongest urge to tuck it behind her ear. "Yeah, I guess if you wouldn't mind helping me tackle the storeroom, that would be great. If you're sure you have time."

A real grin slid across his lips before he could stop himself from looking overly enthusiastic. "Just name a time and it's a date." *Idiot.* "I mean, just tell me when and I'll be here."

"How about tomorrow after work?"

"You got it."

"OK." Madison stood there for a moment, staring at him like he was a disjointed puzzle she couldn't figure out. "Bye." Then she turned on her heel, walked up the back steps of the store, and went inside.

He couldn't help it—he threw a fist pump in the air. Helping another vital business in the community to reopen would look good on his job application for the head community developer position, should it become available as he suspected.

And maybe, at the same time, he'd be able to unravel the mystery of Madison Price. "Challenge accepted."

Evan headed back toward the office. And though he was destined for a night of work and cold meatloaf, he whistled as he walked.

CHAPTER 3

What in the world had made her agree to let Evan Walsh help her with the store?

And why, now that he was here, did her gaze keep drifting back to him? She wished she could blame it on her meticulous nature checking to make sure he was doing things right. But his detailed way of handling everything had settled any lingering concern that he organized like her aunt.

Still, they'd made more progress in one hour than Madison had made earlier today on her own. So whatever her feelings for Evan Walsh, she needed him to stay if she had any hope of clearing this storage room in a timely manner.

"Where do you want this?" His muscles strained beneath his gray T-shirt as he held a box against his chest.

Moonlight trickled in through the singular window, doing a better job of lighting the place than the exposed bulb and old-school chain hanging from the ceiling.

Madison blinked and prayed that he hadn't caught her staring. "What's in it?" Before he could answer, she approached and peeked inside the flaps. "Looks like new hammers."

That lazy grin Madison remembered well returned. "That's what I was going to say."

"You can put them over in that stack." Madison pointed to one of the corners. She flipped to the second page of the clipboard in her hand. "Says here we are low on hammers on the floor, so we should put some out. Can you set about ten aside?"

Evan set down the box. "Not a problem." He dug in and added several hammers to the pile of items to take to the front of the store.

This time, she didn't hide her stare. The Evan Walsh she'd known hadn't been helpful a day in his life. Like the time they'd been part of the same six-person chemistry group sophomore year—he hadn't done a lick of work.

This eager-to-assist man in front of her . . . well, Madison didn't know what to do with him.

He paused, quirking a brow. "What? Do I have spaghetti on my face?"

Yeah, not only was he helping, but he'd arrived tonight with dinner for both of them too. Who was this guy?

"Sorry, I was just thinking about something." Madison put the clipboard down on a box and worked open the flaps of another. "Let's keep going with these."

"You got it." Evan finished the job she'd given him and joined her. A whiff of citrus met her nose. How did the man smell so good after moving boxes for an hour? They'd cracked a window, but the weight of heavy, stale air still hung throughout the room.

She peeked up at him and found him studying her.

"When are you aiming to reopen?"

Madison squatted and pulled a few colorful fishing floats and sinkers from within, some in packaging, some loose. "I'm not sure, exactly. Once I get all the inventory and paperwork organized, I'd like to spruce the place up. Paint it, rearrange a few things, the basics. I'm thinking if I work hard enough, maybe I could have it ready in a few weeks."

"That sounds doable." He helped her sort the fishing tackle by type. "Mondays are out—that's the weekly town council meeting—and I promised my buddy Ben I'd help him do some renovating at his inn this weekend, but I can be here most other nights to help out."

Rocking back on her heels, Madison shook her head. "Wow."

"What?"

"Nothing." An incredulous chuckle fell through her lips. "I just can't get over how much you've changed since high school."

He paused, a quizzical look on his face. "What do you mean?"

She rolled her eyes. "You're not exactly the same guy who tried to cheat off me in our ninth-grade English class."

Through the dim light, she watched his cheeks lose a bit of their color. "We knew each other back then?"

OK, seriously? Madison pursed her lips. "Of course we did." Grabbing the half-full box, she overturned it, allowing a plethora of vibrant colored tackle to spill between them. She refused to look at him as she snatched the yellow plastic worms and fake red fish with hooks attached to the bottom.

"Sorry." Evan's softly spoken word sent a wave of remorse through her. "I have a terrible memory." His hands started to move across the heap in front of them, methodically pulling out green bait and dropping them into a separate pile.

She found it difficult to focus her attention on anything except him.

Blowing hair out of her face, Madison wiped away a bit of perspiration along the top line of her hair. "It's fine."

"Madison." He touched her forearm, and she stilled at the contact.

Her heart galloped as she watched his fingers sitting atop

her skin. Madison couldn't help it. She met his gaze again. The connection nearly took her breath away. "What?"

"I'm pretty good at reading people, but I think even someone who wasn't could probably see that you're upset with me. And given our conversation, I'm guessing it has something to do with the jerk I was in high school."

Madison flinched.

"See?" Evan's hand dropped, and he ran it through his hair, sighing. "Whatever I did to make you dislike me, I'm sorry. It's no excuse, but I really only cared about myself back then. And I drank. A lot."

She probably looked like a fish, but she couldn't help the way her mouth fell open. Never would she have imagined those words coming out of Evan Walsh's mouth.

OK, not *never*. For a brief period during their senior year, she might have believed it of him, back when they'd been secret pen pals through the school's mandatory program. The guy who had written those letters had been sweet, humble, and self-deprecating.

But those letters had ended up being a trick, mere entertainment for the in-crowd that ruled the school, a way to make Madison "Lizard Lady" Price more of a joke than she'd ever been before.

Hadn't they?

No, she wouldn't be fooled again.

Madison clenched her hand into a fist, too late realizing she held an unpackaged lure. She yelped as its hook dug into her palm and grew dizzy at the sight of it embedded there.

Evan hopped to his feet. "Don't move." He ran out of the room.

Madison slumped onto her bottom, staring at the hook. It wasn't painful, exactly—more uncomfortable than anything. Maybe removing it wouldn't be so bad. Carefully, she moved her fingers into position over the hook and gently tugged.

And couldn't help the gasp of pain that gurgled from her throat.

"I told you not to move." Evan came back in the room holding a baggie of ice.

"I thought I could get it out on my own." But the hook still remained fully jabbed into her skin.

He settled onto the ground beside her and grasped her wrist in a light hold, maneuvering her palm into his lap before placing the baggie over the hook. "Yeah, well, sometimes it's OK to ask for help."

Right. Madison had learned a long time ago that, with the exception of Aunt Chrissy, she could only really depend on herself.

Yet as she sat there with Evan holding her hand, looking at her with a crooked smile on his face, she almost wished she could believe his words.

Madison looked back down at her hand. "What's with the ice?"

"We need to keep it on here for about twenty minutes. It'll numb your hand, and then we should be able to remove the hook without any pain."

"So much trouble over a little hook." She cleared her throat. "Thanks, Evan."

"Of course. Couldn't let you stay hooked, now, could we?"

She caught his teasing grin, and a flutter shot through her stomach like a butterfly on steroids. "Well, yes, thank you for taking care of my hand but also for being here. Helping me with the store." A pause. "And for the apology."

Though her palm was starting to numb, it didn't stop her from feeling the faint caress of his thumb over the top of her hand, which he still held steady in his own. "So, what did I do to deserve your wrath?" He kept his tone light, but she sensed the vulnerability in his question.

"Oh." Did he legitimately not know? The look of pained

expectation in his eyes told her that maybe he really didn't remember that moment in junior high when her atrocious nickname had been born.

But how could he have forgotten the very deliberate attempt to mortify her their senior year? She shivered, and it had nothing to do with the ice pressed against her skin.

Because what if the pen pal letters hadn't actually been a trick? What if she'd misinterpreted what had happened that day when they were supposed to meet?

What if he had honestly written those letters without knowing she was the one receiving them?

Then that would mean maybe Evan Walsh had never been as cruel as she'd always made him out to be. Only time would tell.

Running her tongue along her top row of teeth, Madison considered her next words carefully. "It doesn't really matter. You're making up for it now."

"That's nice of you, but seriously. You can tell me. I can take the heat. Believe me, I'm used to it."

"No. I'm not going to be like your dad." She clamped her lips shut but not before she could take back her words.

Evan stiffened. "What did you say?"

"Nothing. How much longer do we need to ice this?"

"I didn't say anything about my dad."

Not now he hadn't, but in those letters? He'd talked more than once about his desire to make his impossible-to-please father proud of him. But she couldn't exactly tell him she remembered that.

"No, yeah, I know. It's just . . . I mean, we all know your dad can be . . . like, he's sometimes . . ." Oh, goodness.

Evan nodded. "Yeah, he is."

"Sorry." Her face flamed. "So, what have you been up to since high school?"

Evan took her change of subject in stride, and they talked for a while about the last ten years, keeping it mostly surface level.

At a lull in the conversation, Evan lifted the half-melted bag of ice from her palm and prodded the skin around the lure. "Do you feel that?"

She shook her head, staring at it. Amazing how she'd almost forgotten about the hook despite the fact it laid buried in her skin. But even so, it had to come out.

The thought made her queasy.

"I'm going to remove this, if that's OK."

She nodded, her eyes not leaving her hand.

"Hey."

Madison glanced up at him. A line seemed to draw them together, invisible but taut.

He offered her a smile. "Relax. Just keep looking at me."

This time, she obliged.

And in ten seconds flat, he squeezed her fingers. "All done."

Just like he'd said it would, the hook had slid right out. "My hero."

She'd meant it jokingly, a way to break the tension. But the way his eyes widened slightly at her words—how he leaned in just a little—made her think maybe, just maybe, she'd unintentionally reeled him closer.

~

Only fifteen more minutes and his workweek would officially end. And for the first time in a long time, he had somewhere he wanted to be.

"Dude."

Evan glanced over at Alex, whose normally serious eyes were bright with amusement. "What?"

"I just said your name, like, five times. Is that budget report really all that interesting, or do you have more pleasant things on your mind?"

"I have no idea what you're talking about." Evan grabbed a

small rubber basketball off his desk then lobbed it toward the small hoop on the back of their office door. It hit the bottom of the net before rolling toward Alex's desk.

Alex picked up the ball and tossed it back to Evan. "So, your distraction has nothing whatsoever to do with the fact I saw your truck outside the hardware store late last night?"

Evan shot the ball again. This time, it swooshed through the net. "I'm just helping out a new friend." And, yeah, trying to add another win in his column so the board would look at him for a promotion—especially now that Denise's job had been posted.

"I'd heard Madison Price had come back to town." Straightening his glasses, Alex lifted his eyebrows. "But are you sure she's just a friend?"

"Of course, man. Nothing else going on." Although Evan had to admit the thought had crossed his mind. The girl was gorgeous and she made sweatpants look good, but there was more to it—something he couldn't explain, something that drew him to her. Once the ice between them had thawed last night—literally and figuratively—he hadn't wanted to leave.

And it had nothing to do with a promotion.

OK. He was in trouble.

"If you say so." Alex paused. "It'd be good, you know. You've been alone for too long."

And that was by choice. Because Evan had spent way too many years using women to get what he wanted, and he didn't want to go back to being that guy. What did Alex know about it? He'd always been on the straight and narrow, the kind of guy with a squeaky-clean reputation and the respect of the whole town to boot. "Look who's talking, dude."

Maybe he could have injected a bit more humor into his tone, but his friend took the jab in stride. "Come on. You've changed, and Madison was always a nice girl. You should go for it, if you like her."

Evan palmed the ball with one hand, running the fingers

from his other along the textured surface. He was considering how to respond when his phone rang. "Saved by the call."

Alex chuckled and turned back to his computer. "For now."

Evan picked up the receiver. "Evan Walsh speaking."

"Evan, this is Hank Aldrin. How are you?"

"I'm good, sir." Why in the world was he calling? After the disappointing meeting on Monday, he hadn't heard a word from anyone at Herman Hardware.

"Glad to hear it. Listen, after a lot of back and forth with the mayor, I wanted to inform you that despite what I said earlier this week, Mr. Herman has narrowed his preferred new locations to three, and Walker Beach is one of them."

Wait, what? Evan sank back in his chair. "Sir, that's—"

"I'm sending Roxy out tomorrow morning to evaluate the proposed site for the store—I'll need you to show her around—and if it suits our needs, we will draw up a contract soon thereafter. I know the mayor is anxious to announce our partnership, so we'll do everything we can on our end to speed the process along."

"That's great, but I need to tell you—"

"I've got to run, but Roxy will be in touch about meeting up tomorrow. Have a good weekend."

The line went dead, and Evan lowered the receiver and groaned.

"Everything OK?" Alex's chair squeaked as he turned.

"I don't know." How had this happened? The company hadn't wanted to settle in a town with a possible competitor. But maybe Dad had convinced Aldrin they didn't have anything to worry about on that account. The mayor had been out of town the last few days, so it was possible he hadn't heard about Madison's decision to reopen the store.

Evan should be happy, right? After all, this is what he'd been working toward for weeks. And it wasn't just good for him, a cred to add to his application for the promotion. It would also be great for the town. As good of a store as Hole-in-the-Wall Hardware had been, Herman would offer lower prices, more jobs, and another reason for people to find themselves downtown. Plus, it would occupy two spaces along the downtown corridor that were currently empty instead of just one.

Yeah, it would be great for everyone—except Madison.

But maybe when she heard about the opportunity with Herman, she'd decide she didn't want to compete. That doing this thing would be harder than she'd thought. And maybe she'd go back to her dream of being a librarian.

Of course, that would take her away from Walker Beach. And the thought of that didn't sit well with him.

"Whatever it is, I'm sorry, man." Alex's voice brought Evan back to the present.

"Just some unsettling news." Evan glanced at the clock—5:02 p.m. His weekend had begun. But he was no longer looking forward to his time with Madison tonight. Because he had to tell her about the possibility of another hardware store coming into town, stealing the livelihood she'd decided to pursue.

Was it too much to hope that she wouldn't hate him for his part in the situation?

After shutting down his computer and snagging his stuff, he wished Alex a good weekend and headed out the door. Half an hour later he stood in front of Chrissy's house holding a semi-hot pizza from Froggies. He'd stopped by the hardware store, but it had been dark and Madison hadn't answered her phone. So he'd wandered here.

Evan knocked and waited. It took a minute, but she finally answered, entirely casual in a thin-strapped shirt that showed off her slender arms and flannel pants that made it look like she'd just rolled out of bed—something he most definitely shouldn't be thinking about. Today her hair was pulled back off her face, and she wore large glasses with thick frames. In her arms she held a big book.

He'd never thought of librarians as particularly sexy, but Madison Price might just change his mind about that.

Her gaze swung from the pizza to Evan's eyes. "Sorry, I lost track of time."

"No problem."

She looked up at him with those liquid chocolate eyes, and all thoughts fled his brain.

"Do you want to come in? We can eat here and then head to the store." Madison widened the door.

He stroked his throat. "Yeah, of course." Memory upon memory hit Evan as he stepped into Chrissy's small house. He hadn't been here much when Chrissy was well, but once she'd gotten too weak to work at the store every day, he'd spent many hours in this very room. And other than a stack of books on the coffee table—Madison's, he presumed, since Chrissy rarely read anything but her Bible—the place looked the same.

The beach decor, the smell of peaches, the overstuffed chair and ottoman with a matching blue couch . . . it all reminded him so much of his mentor and friend. It didn't matter how small the living room. The place welcomed everyone who came inside and made them comfortable while they were there.

Evan held up the pizza. "Where do you want this?"

"On the coffee table is fine. Just move my books if they're in the way." Madison scurried toward the kitchen.

He set down the box and picked the top book off the stack. *Hardware 101.* The others boasted titles like *The All-New Illustrated Guide to Everything Sold in Hardware Stores* and *Small Business for Dummies*. The woman didn't do anything halfway, did she?

Madison re-entered the room with plates and napkins in hand. She plopped next to Evan on the couch and opened the box, inhaling. "I haven't had Froggies in forever. And I'm starving. Thank you for bringing dinner." Separating a piece from the rest of the pie, the cheese stretching and finally tearing away, she plated it and handed it to him before grabbing herself a slice.

"Thanks. And you're welcome." He glanced back at the books. "A bit of light reading you've got going on here."

"Ha. Yes." Taking a bite of the pizza, she sat back against the couch and groaned. "Just as good as I remembered."

Man, how much he wanted to just relax with her, enjoy the pizza, chat about whatever. And he'd be lying if he said he wasn't jealous of the way that slice of pizza got to touch her lips over and over as she ate . . .

But he couldn't enjoy any of it until he'd told her about Herman. After polishing off his slice, he set down his plate and wiped his mouth with a napkin then leaned forward and touched the spine of a book. "So, you're really committing to this, huh?"

"Why wouldn't I? I told you, I don't know anything about running a business, especially a hardware store. So, what I don't know, I read."

"Guess that's the librarian in you talking."

She laughed, the sound igniting his wish that they could talk about anything else right now. That he could just spend the evening getting to know her better. "I guess so." She took another bite of pizza, studying him as she chewed. "When my world is upended, when things don't make sense, I turn to books. I always have. And they've never let me down."

And that was the perfect opening. "Will you be happy running a hardware store, then?"

"What do you mean?"

"You spent the last two years studying to become a librarian. Do you really want to stop pursuing that dream?"

Madison shrugged. "Yes, I thought that would be a great career, but this store has been dropped into my lap. And it's a sure thing. I have bills to pay, and, to be honest, the idea of being subject to a position that's dependent on grant money year in and year out isn't all that appealing."

Great. He was feeling like more of a cad by the minute. "True, but nothing's for sure."

"It almost sounds like you're not happy I'm staying." Her voice came out nearly a whisper, her face softening into a look of expectancy. Then, as if realizing what she'd asked, she blinked hard.

He rushed on. "No, that's not it. But Madison, I can tell you're wicked smart. You can do anything. Are you sure you want to spend your time running your aunt's store?" As soon as the words were out, a desire to punch himself almost took over.

"Excuse me, but I don't remember asking for your approval."

He'd made a mess of this already, and he hadn't even told her everything. Evan massaged the back of his neck. "Sorry, that came out wrong. It's just that there's something I need to tell you, and I wanted to make sure this wasn't some whim, you taking over the store."

"Even if it were a whim, what do you care, Evan?" Gone was the comfortable, relaxed Madison, one replaced by a wary face and crossed arms. "What do you need to tell me?"

"The town is getting close to signing an agreement with a regional hardware chain to open a Walker Beach branch right next door to your store." He winced as the words tumbled out.

For a moment, she didn't say a word, just stared at the pizza box. Had she heard him?

He touched her elbow. "Madison . . ."

She wrenched away and glared at him. Or was that hurt marring her features? Either way, he hated the way she was looking at him. Which was dumb, because even though they'd apparently attended high school together, he'd basically known this woman for four days. Why did he care so much about what she thought?

Closing her eyes, Madison breathed in and out a few times. Finally, she reopened her eyes. "Why didn't you tell me sooner?"

"Until today, I didn't think it was happening."

"So, it's a for sure thing now?"

"Not quite yet but it's one step closer." He explained the process of getting the council to approve the new business in town once Herman agreed to the site. Even though the motion was likely to pass, he wanted to offer her some glimmer of hope. Anything to get the camaraderie from earlier back. "But you remember Bud Travis?"

"Of course. He and his wife owned the Walker Beach Bar & Grill."

"They still do. Anyway, he's been a loud proponent of keeping out any chains, so he may vote against the agreement. He sometimes persuades at least one other council member to vote with him. Occasionally two. If they can get a majority, it may be voted down."

Madison pressed her lips together. "Maybe I should talk to Bud then." She turned her whole body to face him, and he realized how close they were sitting. "Do you think that would be a good idea?"

He swallowed hard. "It couldn't hurt."

"Then that's what I'll do. I'll fight this." Without warning, she grabbed Evan's hand. "And I'm sorry I was a bit taken aback at first. I know you're just looking out for me."

Madison turned his palm over and traced a figure eight in the same spot where he'd removed the hook from hers just last night. "You've been doing that a lot lately. I'm not really used to it."

Oh man. He was a world-class coward, but he definitely couldn't reveal his whole role in the Herman Hardware deal. Not when she was looking at him with trust for the first time. And not when she was so near—inches away, really.

Not when her lips looked impossibly soft and he wanted

nothing more than to lean down and take her in his arms and press his mouth to hers.

"You're welcome." He croaked out the words. His free hand rose of its own accord, skimming her bare shoulder on its way to caress the side of her cheek. "And you're wrong."

Was the apparent surprise on her face from his touch or his words? "About what?"

"You said it sounded like I wasn't happy you were staying. I'm definitely happy." His thumb moved slowly across her lips and, yep, they were softer than he'd imagined. She smelled of vanilla and sunshine, the perfect combination of light and comfort.

"Evan . . ."

Whoa. What was he doing? He dropped his hand. "We should get going. To the store, I mean. If you still want to."

He was an idiot. Yep, total and complete idiot. Madison remembered him from high school, and apparently he'd done something to hurt her. Of course she wouldn't want to get involved with someone like him. He'd probably been imagining the connection between them.

Standing, he hightailed it to the door. But before he could leave, a tug on his sleeve halted his steps. Turning, he found Madison there, eyebrows knit together.

She hugged him and, without thinking, he folded his arms around her. Wow, it felt good . . . her petite frame wrapped tightly against him, fitting there just about perfectly.

Much too quickly, she pulled back and looked up at him. "Thanks, Evan. For being happy. And for all your help."

His stomach twisted. He knew he wasn't good enough for her. But he still couldn't stop himself from wanting to be. "Anytime."

CHAPTER 4

What was happening between her and Evan?

It was a question Madison had asked herself all night as she lay in bed, unable to sleep. Reliving that moment when she'd been sure he was going to kiss her had been the stuff of her high school dreams.

Now, in broad daylight, it seemed like she must have imagined the whole thing.

But she had more pressing things to worry about. Like finding Bud Travis.

Madison tucked a bag of cookies into her purse and strolled down Main Street toward the Walker Beach Bar & Grill. After a few moments of walking, she entered the North Village, where a breeze rippled off the beach between the buildings. This area of town had always been somewhat trendier, with a lot of organic and vegan options. Most of the boutiques and restaurants—like the coffee-ice-cream-combo shop Java's Village Bean and Oil Me This, a store that sold specialty olive oils and vinegars—were somewhat new or had come in sometime during the ten years that Madison had been absent.

But here, evidence of the earthquake that had hit six months ago still reigned. CLOSED FOR REPAIRS signs hung above several storefronts, and a few businesses had collapsed roofs or were still boarded up.

And there was the library, its front stone steps completely crumbled, a blue tarp over the roof. Madison's heart squeezed as she peeked inside the blackened windows. She couldn't see much more than the shelving units that, as a child, she'd known like the back of her hand. This place had brought more comfort to a young, hurting girl than the librarian could ever have known.

Madison ran her fingers along the dusty window, a memory coming to mind of what had started as a typical day in seventh grade, about a year after she'd moved in with Aunt Chrissy. Somehow, she'd managed to go the whole time without making a single friend. Sure, some kids had been nice to her, but they'd all eventually labeled Madison as odd simply because she preferred books to people. Of course, it had taken several years of counseling for her to realize that not everyone was going to leave her like her parents had, that fictional people could only provide a certain level of comfort, and that she needed actual people in her life.

But on this particular day, she'd been determined to make it through lunch without reading, praying that maybe if she kept up her head, she'd make a friend.

As she passed Roxy Chamberlain's table, occupied by all the kids with designer clothing and flawless skin, Madison attempted to smile at them.

And ran right into Roxy's boyfriend, Evan Walsh. The whole room exploded with laughter.

Madison glanced down at her white shirt—now covered in the spaghetti from her lunch tray.

What had she been thinking to come in here? She should have eaten lunch in the bathroom like every other day.

Roxy sidled up beside Evan. "Nice one."

Evan's gaze was on Madison, but he seemed to look right through her. "I didn't even see her."

"Well, that's because her shirt is the same color as the walls."

Not anymore, it wasn't. Oh, she had to get out of here before she embarrassed herself anymore by vomiting on Roxy and Evan.

Evan smirked like it was all a big joke. And to him, it probably was. "She's like . . . camouflaged. Like a chameleon."

Move, Madison. Move. *But her feet just wouldn't cooperate.*

"Oh, that's perfect. She does kind of resemble a lizard with that dry, patchy skin. Ever heard of moisturizer, Lizard Lady?"

The peel of Roxy's laughter joined with a chorus of jocks chanting "Lizard Lady." Evan just stood there, looking between Roxy and Madison, until Madison finally managed to make a mad dash for the exit.

Madison had run here, to the public library, where she'd huddled in the corner with a copy of *Anne of Green Gables*. How well she'd related to the misfit orphan—a girl who'd had to learn to stand up for herself.

"Madison?"

She jolted, turning on her heel.

Ashley Baker stood on the sidewalk with a tall blond man and a curvy woman sporting stylish brown hair streaked with highlights. "You OK?"

"Just reminiscing about the library. I can't believe the shape it's in."

"Sad, right?" Ashley indicated the man and woman next to her. "You remember my brother Ben, don't you? He owns our family's inn just north of town now. And this is his girlfriend, Bella. She's the inn's manager. Guys, this is Madison, a friend from high school."

Lean and athletic like his sister, Ben was several years older. Of course Madison remembered him. What girl hadn't had a crush on Ben Baker at some point? "How are you?"

Ben slid his arm across Bella's shoulders and nodded at Madison. "Good to see you again."

Bella smiled warmly. "It's so nice to meet you."

"I wish we could chat, but we're meeting our parents for lunch." Ashley tilted her head. "Madison, I heard through the grapevine that you may be staying in Walker Beach. Is that true?"

She'd forgotten how quickly word traveled in a small town. "Yeah, actually. I'm excited."

Ashley squealed, clapping her hands. "That's amazing! I miraculously have some free time in my schedule next week if you want help with anything."

After working a few extra hours last night, Evan and Madison had made decent progress on the inventory, but there was still so much to do. Especially if Herman Hardware was going to come into the picture . . .

Speaking of that, she needed to get on with her mission for today before she did anything else.

"Thanks. I may take you up on that."

"And now that you're staying, I'll definitely be bugging you about helping me with my library project." Ashley winked.

That actually sounded like a nice distraction, albeit one she couldn't afford right now. "Yeah, maybe once I've reopened the store." Madison checked her watch. "I'll call you, OK?"

"Great." After a quick hug, Ashley walked off with her brother and Bella.

Madison hurried toward the bar and grill, one of the northern-most storefronts on Main Street. She ducked inside, the smell of grilled burgers and onions overtaking her. Big-screen TVs playing different sports channels lined the walls. Patrons were scattered around the room, eating and laughing. Outside, a patio extended onto the beach, granting visitors a gorgeous view of the foamy ocean and California coast rising to the north. That's where Madison headed.

Fewer people sat on the deck, but there, in the corner where he'd always eaten his Saturday lunch, no matter the weather, sat Bud Travis. Though he was ten years older, the spry seventy-something looked almost the same as he always had, with his diminished hairline, high cheekbones, long white beard, and tan skin. On his plate rested a few bites of the grill's calamari sandwich—Bud's favorite as long as Madison had known him.

At her approach, he looked up from the book he was reading and flashed her a grin. "Well, I'll be. Is that Ms. Maddie Price?"

Madison couldn't help but return the smile. "Hey, Mr. Travis."

"You're all grown up, so it's Bud to you now." Winking, he held out his hand.

She gripped it and leaned down for a hug. "I'm not sure I can do that."

"Mr. Bud, then."

Why had she waited nearly a week to find him and say hello? At least she'd remembered how much he'd always enjoyed Chrissy's carrot cake cookies. She pulled them from her bag and held them out. "I come bearing gifts."

Whistling, he took the bag and opened it, inhaling the scent of the fresh-baked treats. "My, how I've missed that smell. Please say you'll sit and share a few."

"I may have already eaten my weight in them. But I would love to join you regardless." Madison pulled out the chair across from him and sat facing Bud. In the distance, she glimpsed the lighthouse that was only five miles north of Walker Beach. "How are you? And how's Velma?"

"We're both fine, just fine. And how are you, Ms. Maddie? I'm sorry about your aunt."

"Thank you. I'm good. Actually, I'm . . ." She bit her lip. "I'm moving back. To run the store."

"I'd heard that." A small frown tugged Bud's lips downward. "Well, that's great news." He took a cookie in hand and stared at it but didn't make a move toward eating.

"You don't look like it's great news." She studied him. "Because of Herman Hardware?"

"You know about that, eh?" Wrinkles she hadn't noticed before became more prominent on Bud's forehead as he scowled. "I'm sorry, Maddie-Girl. I don't mean to be a downer. You know me. I'll be voting against it. Stores like that don't have Walker Beach's best in mind. They only care about the bottom line, not people. Not like your Aunt Chrissy did. But my voice doesn't carry much weight around here anymore." Finally, he nibbled the cookie.

"I'm sure that's not true." She reached across the table and squeezed his wrinkled hand. "You're well-respected by everyone."

His gaze narrowed. "Not everyone. To a lot of people, I'm just an old codger, too set in my ways—in the traditions of the past—to allow progress. And maybe I am. But there's something to be said for tradition." Snagging his napkin, he swiped cookie crumbs from the corners of his mouth.

She let go of his hand and grabbed a cookie for herself. "Well, I know of at least one other government employee who will do all he can to oppose the agreement." Evan hadn't come out and said as much, but with his job, he had to hold some influence. And after the way he'd treated her last night, she couldn't imagine him not lending his full support. "If we could sway just a few more council members to our side, the motion will fail, and Herman Hardware will leave our little town alone."

Grunting, Bud quirked a bushy eyebrow. "And just who would the other employee be? The committee is keeping it fairly hush-hush for now, and as far as I know, I'm the only one against it."

"Evan Walsh." Breaking the cookie, she popped a piece in her mouth. The cream cheese frosting melted against her tongue. Aunt Chrissy really had been a genius when it came to her cookies.

After she swallowed, she noticed a strange look on Bud's face. "What?"

"Evan Walsh, you said?"

"Yes."

"He's the one who spearheaded the whole agreement from the beginning. It's his father's pet project."

She pressed her fingers against the remaining cookie in her hand. It crumbled, falling onto the wooden table. "Are you sure?" There had to be a mistake. Evan would have said something.

Or maybe she'd fallen prey to his charms. Again. But why would he betray her?

Her head hurt.

"Sure as I am that the sky is blue."

Madison was glad someone was sure of something, because right now, she didn't know what to believe. Who was Evan Walsh, really? Was he friend or foe?

The only thing Madison *was* sure of? She wasn't in high school anymore.

And this time, she was getting to the bottom of Evan's deception, whether he liked it or not.

~

He'd rather be anywhere but here.

Evan stood in the middle of the empty storefront next door to Hole-in-the-Wall Hardware, hands in his pockets, waiting for Roxy to finish looking around. Definitely not how he wanted to spend his Saturday morning.

His eyes trailed her as she snapped photos on her iPhone from every angle. Decked out in her usual designer garb—tight jeans and a blouse that hugged her curvy frame and didn't leave much to the imagination—Roxy's heels clicked on the rustic wooden floor coated with dust. A souvenir shop had previously occupied the space, evidenced by circular metal clothing racks still dispersed throughout the store. The smell of wood polish lingered in the air.

Finally, Roxy shoved her phone back into her purse and approached him. "Thanks again for meeting me on such short notice." She pumped her fingers through the roots of her bleached blond hair.

"No problem." He should be at Ben's inn, helping out like he'd promised. As soon as they were done, he'd head over. But while he was here, he might as well pick Roxy's brain. "So what do you think? Will this space work?"

Roxy scrunched her nose in that way she'd had since they were kids when she didn't know an answer. "That's above my pay grade." She ran her manicured hands along the wooden counter at the back of the store, lifted a finger, and grimaced at the layer of dirt now hanging out there. "But I do know that they're excited about this deal. And so am I."

"Why is that?" Evan ducked behind the counter, located a rag, and handed it to her.

She grabbed it from him without acknowledgment and wiped off her hand. "They see a lot of potential in this location. And I'm excited because I get a nice bonus for making the deal happen. A possible promotion too."

"Glad to hear it." Now, how to ask the question he really wanted answered? "So, what would happen if, say, the current hardware store was to reopen?"

Roxy tossed the rag onto the floor and placed her hands on her hips. "Your dad assured us that the current owner wasn't staying."

"Let's be hypothetical about it, then."

"Fine. *Hypothetically,* Aldrin may decide to pull out of the agreement if the old store is a big enough threat." Advancing, Roxy now stood nearly toe-to-toe with Evan. The tropical perfume that he'd always found so intoxicating nearly suffocated him. "So, Evan, how big is the threat?"

How did he answer that? Was Madison's store really going to threaten Herman Hardware? The opposite seemed much more likely. But he didn't want to count her out. He saw the determination in her, the feisty desire to learn what she didn't know. And Walker Beach's residents might be loyal to her simply because she was Chrissy's niece.

"I think the new owner has a legitimate chance at making a go of it."

"Who's the new owner?" Roxy's thin eyebrows raised.

She didn't know? Then again, she probably had much better things to do with her time than to stay current with the Walker Beach gossip. "Madison Price."

Recognition filtered through Roxy's fake eyelashes, and she snorted. "Madison Price? You think *she* has a chance of running a successful business?"

He frowned. "Why not?"

"Don't you remember her from high school?"

"No." Although according to Madison, he should have.

"Seriously? How could you forget Lizard Lady?"

"Wait. That was *her*?" He ran a hand through his hair. "I didn't know that."

"How could you not? You're the one who gave her the nickname in the first place."

"No, I didn't." He paused. "Did I?"

"Well, it was both of us." Roxy rolled her eyes. "I'm not surprised you don't remember. You were still hungover from Duncan McAllister's party the night before."

Story of his life. He shook his head. "No wonder she hated me when we first met." He snatched the rag Roxy had dropped and set it back where he'd found it.

"Oh, that's adorable."

"What?" He glanced at her and found a mocking stare looking straight at him.

"You like her."

Evan was done with this conversation. Turning, he headed for the front door. "You got your pictures. Let's get out of here."

Roxy didn't move. "Fine then. Maybe you don't like her. I don't really care. All I care about is you not wrecking this deal for me. I've worked too hard—at a company full of men who think they're God's gift to women, by the way—to sacrifice this promotion because you've decided to go soft over a girl you haven't seen in ten years."

"I told you. I don't even remember her."

"It sounds like she remembers you."

The storefront's key dug into his palm as he fisted it. "We may not have been friends, but I never made fun of her. You were the one who insisted on calling her names."

"You didn't exactly rush to her defense, though, did you? And she won't easily forget that, believe me."

She pulled her purse strap tighter against her shoulder and strutted toward him, one short punctuated heel clop after another.

Blowing out a breath, Evan wrenched open the door and walked into the brisk outdoor air, breathing in the briny scent of ocean water. He waited a few moments before losing his patience. "Come on, Roxy. I need to lock up."

She took her sweet time getting out of there. As he locked the door, she studied the front of Hole-in-the-Wall Hardware. "You know, three storefronts would probably be more to Aldrin's liking. He really wants this store to make an impact."

"That one isn't available."

Ignoring him, she pulled her phone out again and took a few more photos of the three storefronts next to each other. "For now."

She shoved the phone back into her purse and snagged a

pair of large white sunglasses, which she placed on the bridge of her nose. She peered over Evan's shoulder, a smile curling over her lips. Then, without warning, she pushed up on her heels and kissed him on the cheek.

"What the . . ." His brain told him to wrench away, but she was stepping back before he could.

Roxy chuckled. "I hope Herman Hardware can count on you to get the job done." Then she turned on her heel and left.

Evan rubbed the back of his neck. What had just happened?

"Well, that was just precious."

Madison? He whirled and found her there, face contorted, her petite frame seeming much taller than it had just yesterday. "That wasn't what it looked like."

"I don't really care what it looked like, Evan. All I care about is the truth."

"I'm telling you the truth."

Madison folded her arms. "So why were you hanging out with Roxy Chamberlain, then?"

Great. He was cornered. If he admitted he was showing Roxy the open space downtown, he might have to tell Madison about his involvement in the Herman Hardware deal.

He could lie, tell her that Roxy was just in the neighborhood, had wanted to reconnect as old friends.

But no. Evan was done with that way of life. Lies only brought heartache. Which meant he needed to come clean. But how, when Madison's eyes flashed like a summer storm with a mind of its own? "Uh—"

"Is it all a game to you, Evan? Do you even . . ." Madison huffed, biting her lip, and her eyes grew glassy for a moment before she rubbed the end of her nose.

He stepped nearer, but she moved backward. It was only then that he noticed a few people watching them as they passed on the sidewalk. Evan inclined his head toward Madison and lowered his voice. "You want to discuss this inside? I can whip up a few cups of coffee on Chrissy's old coffeemaker. Remember how she—"

"Don't." Madison ground out the word between clenched teeth. "Stop talking about her as if you cared. It's so obvious that you don't. Bud Travis told me everything. About Herman Hardware. How you're the one actually behind it all. How long have you had this in the works? And how could you do that to Aunt Chrissy? You planned to run her out of business, all while pretending to be her friend."

"No, you have it all wrong, Madison."

But she wasn't listening. "And you and Roxy, well, you were probably having a great laugh at my expense. Again." Fumbling with her keys, Madison's hands shook as she inserted the right one into the door and twisted the knob. It didn't open and she banged her hand on the frame, pressing her forehead against it in defeat. "Just go, Evan."

Evan reached for the handle and gently twisted it. The door gave way. "Madison, please."

"Fool me once, shame on you. Fool me twice, though . . ."

He could understand why she'd think he'd fooled her this time, but when else had she felt that way? It must have something to do with what he'd done to her in high school.

His fingers pulsed with the need to punch the wall. Would his past ever let go of him? "Can we please just talk?"

"So you can lie to me some more?" Madison pushed the door wider. "I don't know why you've chosen me as the butt of your jokes, but I'm tired of it. We're adults now. Try acting like it."

The door slammed in his face.

CHAPTER 5

She realized too late that she'd chosen paint the same color as Evan's eyes.

Madison pushed the paint can across the counter and groaned.

"What's wrong?" Ashley looked up from the wall she was taping behind the counter. Her height gave her an advantage over Madison, and apparently, she simply adored home improvement type projects. Was there anything the woman wasn't good at?

"Just not sure I like the paint I picked."

"For the accent wall?" At Madison's nod, Ashley turned and pried the lid off the can nearest to her. "I like it. It's bright and bold and welcoming. It'll be the perfect color."

During the last three days, Madison had worked nonstop to tidy up the store, getting inventory situated and the books in order. There was still more to do, but she needed a break from staring at the numbers—thus, why she'd invited Ashley to help spruce up the front of the store. Painting was the first logical step. Then she could tidy the space, restock, and dust and polish a final time. After that, she'd be ready for business.

Well, as ready as she'd ever be.

"OK." Madison didn't have time to order more paint or travel to the nearest town to buy a different color anyway. If she wanted to stay on schedule to reopen in less than two weeks—an ambitious but doable goal—then today was painting day.

"Let's do this." Madison turned Aunt Chrissy's old radio on low to provide some musical motivation while they worked.

Ashley finished taping the walls while Madison poured the paint into paint pans and readied the brushes. They each grabbed a roller and started to turn the massive accent wall blue.

"How is your job going?" Madison leaned into the roller, attempting to ignore how the aqua made the wall come to life before her eyes.

"It's good. Pretty busy right now. Last weekend was rare. From now until the end of the summer, I probably won't have much of a break." Ashley dipped her roller into the paint, which globbed onto the end of the foam.

"And you like it?"

"Yeah, it's great. I have a boss who works me hard, but he's fair. I've learned a lot from him."

"Are you still planning to open your own wedding planning business someday? Wasn't that always your dream?"

Funny. Madison had never considered herself entrepreneurial but just look at her now.

"You have a good memory. And yeah, that's what I've always wanted to do, but it would take money and time. Between work and the library board and family obligations, I don't have much of either one right now." Ashley ran her roller over the wall in smooth, even strokes, the picture of serenity. "But I'm gaining experience in event coordination and building a reputation. And those things are important when running a business."

And they were two things Madison didn't have at all. Yet here she was, thinking she could reboot a business her family had successfully run for fifty-something years. All because she'd read a few books.

She set down the roller and picked up a brush for edging. Attempting to copy Ashley's calm movements, she pushed the brush up and down, but her hand trembled.

Evan's words from last weekend floated back to her. *"You spent the last two years studying to become a librarian. Do you really want to stop pursuing that dream?"*

The truth was she'd asked herself the same question. But no, she'd made the decision to stay, and she needed to stick it out. She couldn't allow him—who'd clearly had an ulterior motive—to get into her head.

"So, what's going on with you and Evan Walsh?"

"Excuse me?" Madison's hand swiped the tape, nearly hitting the wrong wall.

"You heard me, girl. People talk. Apparently, you two had quite the argument on Saturday."

Madison took a deep breath. Now she remembered why she hated small towns. When she'd lived in Los Angeles, people had barely noticed her, but here, everything she did was under a microscope.

Dipping the brush back into the paint, she jerked her wrist, feeling a strange satisfaction at the way bits of paint smacked the wall. "I found out that he hasn't changed as much as I thought he had." She smoothed the globs of paint into streaks that blended in with the rest.

"What do you mean?"

The upbeat tune on the radio faded into some sappy love song. Madison flipped to another station. Country music poured out, and a female artist sang about getting revenge on her cheating ex. She turned the volume up a notch.

Then she filled Ashley in on the situation with Herman Hardware. "It's dumb, really. I somehow convinced myself that he cared about helping me get the store in the right shape. That maybe he cared about me."

To be fair, he'd never come out and said he cared about her or that he wanted more than friendship—or even that he wanted friendship, really. She'd just assumed. But there had been that moment when it seemed like he might kiss her. . . .

What was she thinking? Evan Walsh was a guy used to getting any woman he wanted. Probably even those he didn't really want too. "I forgot that he's just a player and world-class jerk to boot."

Ashley stopped painting and set her eyes upon Madison. "He's actually changed a lot in the last several years."

"Really? How?"

"For one, he's got a solid job and works really hard. He hasn't dated anyone in a long time. And he used to be a regular at the Canteen—it's a karaoke bar in the North Village—but I haven't seen him there in a while. Not that I'm there a ton, but I heard it was like his second home for years."

Madison took a deep breath, but the strong smell of paint filled her nostrils. She coughed then set down her brush and stepped away from the wall, studying it. The first coat was nearly complete, and Ashley was right—it was bold, bright. But it was only the first coat. After a second, the color would positively shine.

Funny how comparison could denigrate what seemed good now. "It doesn't matter, anyway. He has his life, and I have mine. Our paths were never really meant to intersect. We're from different worlds."

"What's that supposed to mean? You're both from Walker Beach." Ashley rested her brush on the tray and joined Madison at the counter.

Ashley would never understand. She had always been buddy-buddy with everyone—it's how she'd ended up being one of Madison's only friends. But she also had one of those personalities that people gravitated toward.

Kind of like Evan.

"Never mind." She offered Ashley a wet wipe then snagged one for herself, dragging it along the edges of her fingers.

Ashley followed suit. "You wouldn't be so upset with him if you didn't like him, you know."

Madison shut her eyes and wished she could do the same with her ears. But Ashley was right. Somehow, in an embarrassingly short time, Evan Walsh had weaseled his way back into her heart. She'd have to make sure the doors were shut extra tight this time. Because even though he'd lied—or, at the very least, omitted the entire truth—she'd still found herself wanting to hear him out since Saturday.

Of course, she'd ignored his texts and hadn't answered the door the few times he'd come by since then. How mature of her. But what else could a girl do? Clearly her judgment around him was not what it should be.

Sighing, Madison slumped against the counter. "Yeah, I know. And I feel like such an idiot for it."

"You're not." Ashley came closer and threw an arm around Madison, squeezing her shoulders before letting go. "You keep saying he hasn't changed. I know he wasn't the most well-behaved kid in high school, but it sounds like there's more to the story."

Her friend would think Madison was pathetic for still caring about this ten years later. And really, she didn't, but it went to a pattern of behavior she should have seen coming. "There is."

"And it sounds like the kind of story that requires chocolate." Ashley turned on her heel and marched through the back doorway toward the room that served as a mini kitchen.

OK, then. Madison followed and found Ashley rummaging in the few cupboards over the sink. Next to that sat the microwave. "What are you looking for?"

"Ah. Here we go." Ashley produced two oversized mugs—a turquoise one painted with Kokopelli, the other boasting the Luke's Diner label from the TV show *Gilmore Girls*. "Now to find the hot chocolate."

"All the way to the left."

Ashley found the packets of Nestlé's cocoa and filled each mug with water before sticking them into the microwave. The beeping of the buttons filled the silence between them.

This was Madison's kitchen now. She should be the one making cocoa for her friend. But all she had the energy for was to plop down at the bright green two-person table while Ashley pulled the mugs of barely boiling water onto the counter and filled them with the chocolate powder.

"So." She side-glanced at Madison while she stirred, the metal spoon clanking against the porcelain mug. "What's the story?"

How long had it been since Madison had confided in anyone? Too long. But suddenly, she craved a connection. So when Ashley offered her the mug of steaming chocolate, Madison took it. "Thank you."

"No problem." Ashley slid into the seat across from her, blowing on her own drink.

"No, really, Ash." Madison picked up her cup. The first sip burned the tip of her tongue and roof of her mouth. She blew, took another, and allowed her shoulders to relax. "Thank you."

A small smile curved over Ashley's lips. "My pleasure. Now spill. The story, not the drink."

Madison laughed. "So, remember that pen-pal program we had to participate in during senior year?"

"Oh yeah. That was kind of cool in concept. But whoever I was paired with was a real slacker." Ashley took a drink. "I think I only got one or two letters from her all semester."

"You never found out who you had, huh?"

"No." Ashley scrunched her nose. "Were we supposed to?"

"Not necessarily. I think it was a secret for a reason. So you could be 'your most honest self.'" At first, Madison hadn't been. She couldn't remember exactly what that first letter to her pen pal had said, just the feel of it. Because there was no way she was opening her most private thoughts up to a stranger.

But then, something had happened. Her pen pal had been gut-wrenchingly honest. At least, she'd thought so at the time. And that had nudged something inside of her to do the same.

"Wait." As Ashley sat straighter, the legs of her chair scraped the floor. "Did you find out your pen pal's identity?"

"Yes."

"How?"

"We . . ." Madison averted her eyes, studying the popcorn texture of the ceiling as if it were the most fascinating thing in the world. "Over the four months that we exchanged letters, we started writing to each other more and more frequently. I must have dropped a letter in the box every other day from March on. Just before graduation, my pen pal suggested we meet." She glanced back at Ashley, who leaned forward, her mug pushed aside.

"And?"

"And so we arranged a time. I got held up after school with a group project and was a bit late in meeting. When I got to Froggies—" She bit her lip, remembering how her stomach had twisted, her jaw dropped. "It was the last person I thought it'd be."

"It was Evan, wasn't it?"

"Yes."

"What happened?"

"I stood there staring at him for what seemed like forever. I'd almost gotten up the nerve to say hi, but then Roxy and her gang walked in behind me."

Madison had been so intent on watching Evan, she hadn't noticed until Roxy threw her arm around Madison's shoulder and leaned in close to whisper, *"As if he'd ever be into a nobody like you, Lizard Lady."*

She pulled herself out of the memory to refocus on Ashley. "The look on her face, the way all of them laughed . . . I knew I'd been duped."

"Duped?"

"Obviously, they'd found out I was Evan's pen pal and thought it'd be hilarious to humiliate me. I mean, he wrote all sorts of things that made me think—" She slammed back the rest of her hot chocolate, which, she was relieved to notice, was no longer scalding. "Anyway, it doesn't matter anymore. It just means I should have known better than to let myself like him now."

Ashley folded her lip between her teeth for a brief moment. "Have you given Evan a chance to explain himself? About the hardware store *and* the past?"

"Not exactly."

"I mean, I get it. It does sound like he wasn't totally truthful about the hardware store, but maybe he has his reasons. Or maybe things aren't what they seem like. You'll never know if you don't hear him out."

Madison groaned. Ashley had a point. "I'll think about it."

CHAPTER 6

Dad was going to be furious.

Evan hung up the phone and scrubbed a hand across his face.

He'd been waiting all week to hear from Hank Aldrin after informing him on Monday about Madison's plans to reopen Hole-in-the-Wall Hardware, but the man had been radio-silent —probably to leave Evan to sweat it out. Now, it was Friday morning, and Hank had finally let him know the contract was a no-go if there was a competitor in town.

Evan paced. Alex was out today, so he was alone in the office for once. Too bad. He could have used a friend about now—or a buffer at the very least. Any minute, Dad would burst through that door. He'd blame Evan, though Evan had no idea how he could have prevented this. It's not like he had any control over what Madison did.

And now that she wouldn't talk with him, he couldn't even claim credit for helping the hardware store to reopen, which left a big fat blank on the achievements section of his resume where there should have been a major win for the town. Applications for Denise's job were due next week, and he'd be at a disadvantage with this looming over him.

Not that he blamed Madison for not talking to him. Evan hadn't told her the whole truth. He'd messed up big time. Again.

But that didn't stop him from missing her, and his regret tasted even more bitter for it.

A knock sounded on the door. Evan shook himself out of his momentary stupor and braced for a barrage of familiar disappointment. "Come in."

The door creaked as it opened in painfully slow motion. But instead of his father, Madison stood in the doorway.

Evan pivoted, knocking his knee against his desk. He cringed as the bang resounded through the office and pain radiated through his leg. "Madison. Hi." Wow, he sure sounded intelligent. What was it about this woman that made him so nervous? "How are you? Come in."

"Hey, Evan." She folded her arms across her chest, and her right fingers held her left upper arm in a death grip. "Actually, I was hoping we could go for a walk. Or just . . . out. Somewhere."

"Absolutely." *Don't sound so eager.* He slowed his pace as he shut down his computer, snagged his phone and keys, and walked toward the doorway. "There's a nice patio with tables and chairs off the back of the building."

"OK."

After locking up, he led Madison down the hallway, waving hello and nodding greetings to several local politicians and city employees as they passed. Soon, they came to the door that led to the patio dotted with wire tables and chairs. Being nearly lunchtime and a warm sixty-five degrees or so, most seats were taken, but he located an empty table toward the back and indicated that Madison should follow him.

City Hall was one of the main structures—and one of the most longstanding—on Main Street in the historic district, and it backed to the lush green hills. Tall pines dotted the landscape in front of them, offering a spectacular view of the rolling scenery. Birds twittered somewhere above, and the sound of the ocean crashed and swelled in the distance.

He pulled out a chair for Madison then took a seat across from her, though not before he caught a whiff of her sweet-scented shampoo. "What did you want to talk about?" His words fought to release against the tacky pull of his tongue. Man, he could go for a glass of water right now.

The breeze tugged at Madison's hair, and a few wisps caught against her pink lips. "I know you've been trying to get ahold of me this week. To . . . explain things." She sighed as she fiddled with her light scarf. "A friend suggested I hear you out. So, here I am."

Evan coughed through a lump in his throat. He didn't deserve a chance to explain, but she was giving him one anyway. "Thank you, Madison." How to begin? He studied her hands, wishing he could reach out and take them in his own. But that might scare her away. It's not like she knew him well or what he was thinking or feeling. And any trust in him she might have had had been shattered.

He placed his hands flat on the table. "I'm really sorry for hurting you. And I'm not going to pretend that I didn't purposefully keep certain information from you, but it's not for the reasons you may think."

She quirked an eyebrow but didn't say anything.

"I started pursuing the agreement with Herman after Chrissy died. Please believe me, I would never ever have entertained the idea if she'd been alive or if I'd known that you'd be coming back and want to reopen the store."

"But now that I am? And I do?"

"I actually just found out that the agreement is dead in the water, so it's a nonissue."

"Really?"

"Really." He paused. "But even if they did decide to open a

branch here, I think, well, if anyone could succeed at something out of their depth, it would be you."

Madison opened her mouth as if to say something then closed it again. Her jaw flexed. "Why do you say that?" Her voice trembled as the words spilled out.

He couldn't help himself anymore—he placed his hands over hers, and while she stiffened, she didn't pull away. He waited for her to look him in the eyes before speaking again. "Your aunt always told me you could do anything you put your mind to. And I just have this gut feeling that there's a lot more to you than I even know."

She just stared at him for a moment. The scent of pine rolled from the hills, surrounding them. Finally, she spoke. "I have a feeling there's a lot more to you too."

"Would you give me a chance? To find out?" He cringed as the longing spilled into the question.

"What do you mean?"

Evan squared his shoulders, preparing for rejection. "I'd like to take you out. Tomorrow, if you're free."

"I don't know, Evan. I want to believe that you didn't mean to hurt me. . . ."

But his own reputation preceded him. Roxy's words from last weekend taunted him. *"You didn't exactly rush to her defense either, though, did you? And she won't easily forget that."*

Should he just walk away, hands given up in defeat?

Instead, he squeezed Madison's fingers. "Just one date. You can ask me anything, and I promise to answer truthfully. Then you can determine for yourself what you think of me."

She swallowed hard, the smooth skin along her neck rippling with the motion. "I guess Chrissy believed in you. So, OK."

"OK?" He couldn't help the laugh that stumbled from his mouth.

"Yes. OK." She checked her watch then stood. "Text me

details, if you don't mind. I have to go. I've got a meeting at the bank to discuss Aunt Chrissy's—well, my—finances."

"Will do. And Madison? Thanks."

She stood, unsmiling. "I'll see you tomorrow." Turning, she headed back inside, leaving Evan sitting there smiling like a fool.

"What was that all about, son?"

His dad's voice startled him out of his thoughts about where to take Madison on their date. Looking up, he found the mayor standing there, a boxed salad in hand.

"What? Oh. Nothing." Evan held Dad's stare.

"Is that the girl causing all the trouble? The reason Hank Aldrin just called me in a rage?"

Evan wanted to call out Dad for his clear derision when speaking about Madison. But he wouldn't engage. Lot of good that would do. "Yes, that's Madison Price."

Dad sat in the seat Madison had vacated. "I overheard you making plans to take her out."

"Yes." The mayor would think him a traitor. Well, too bad.

His dad studied him a moment then nodded. "I have to admit, Evan, I didn't think you had it in you. I'm impressed."

Wait, what?

His dad ignored the perplexed look Evan was giving him and opened his salad, squirting the packet of Ranch dressing all over the lettuce greens. With a lowered voice, he continued. "You saw what needs to be done, and you figured out how to accomplish it, no matter the personal cost to yourself. That takes guts, son. And I admire you for it."

"And what is it that needs to be done?"

Stabbing a cherry tomato, his dad brought it to his mouth. "We want her to recognize that opening her store is a mistake, of course. That it's selfish for her to take away the jobs and lowered prices that her fellow townspeople could enjoy if Herman Hardware provided for the home improvement needs of the town. And who better to do that than someone she's dating, who she trusts? Bravo, son. I'm confident you'll get us what we want in no time." He bit into the tomato, and some of the juice dribbled onto his lips. He quickly swiped away the mess.

Evan couldn't help staring at him. How could his father think he'd do that to a woman?

Ironic, really. Because that's the man he was trying really hard not to be anymore. And his dad had made it clear that *that* man had been an embarrassment, a disappointment.

His head hurt. His dad had referred to what they "wanted," but with every interaction, it was becoming clearer to Evan that he wanted Madison. But he also wanted that promotion.

And he was starting to wonder if it were possible to have both.

CHAPTER 7

How had Evan known to come here?

Madison climbed from the truck, breathless as she looked out across Baker Community Park. What started as a field of grass boasting a children's playground and barbecue pits became sand then sea. The ha-ha-ha of seagulls echoed from the ocean as the birds swooped against the waves and beach searching for their next meal. On either side of the six-acre park, brown bluffs rose to meet the horizon. Waves pummeled the rocks, which escalated at a gentle slope, forming natural seats along the way.

Perfect for watching the show below.

Evan stood next to her clutching the truck door. Even in his casual pullover sweater and jeans, he was achingly handsome, but the most adorable thing about him was the uncertain yet hopeful expression that lit his face. "Your aunt talked about this place a lot, so I thought—"

"It's perfect." She closed her eyes for a moment, breathing in the tangy scent of salt-tinged air. Then she opened them and found Evan watching her. Blood rushed to her cheeks as she stepped aside so he could shut the door. "Where to?"

He reached into the backseat and pulled out a blanket and basket. Wow. A picnic? She had figured they'd just hit a place in town for lunch, but this was so much better.

"I scoped out a place up that way last night, if it isn't taken yet." He pointed toward the southern set of bluffs.

They started off across the landscape, which at ten in the morning wasn't terribly crowded yet. The weather was due to warm up later today, but for now, Madison burrowed down in her sweatshirt, grateful she'd thought to toss it on over her long-sleeved blouse before Evan had shown up. The ground softened into sand, and grains fell over the sides of her Keds.

Finally, they arrived at the bluff and climbed the rocks until they were about halfway up—high enough to see the horizon but not too far from the water.

"How is this?"

"It's great." But surely he knew that. "You've gone whale watching before, haven't you?"

"Nope." Evan spread the blanket onto the rocks, which were scattered with bits of sand and pebbles. "Most of my family outings were sports-related. All of our free time was spent attending my sister's gymnastics meets or my baseball games."

"How is Taylor these days?" Lowering herself onto the blanket, Madison hugged her legs against her chest.

Evan scooted the picnic basket next to the blanket then joined her in sitting. "She won Miss California about five years ago, lives in Los Angeles, and works as a social media influencer." He slung his arms across his bent knees, right arm holding his left wrist.

"What a life."

"Yeah. My parents are really proud of her." A muscle flexed in Evan's jaw.

"I'm sure they're proud of you too." Whatever his motivations, one thing was clear—he was no longer the lazy goof-off from high school.

Evan shrugged. "My mom has said so, but my dad's another story. I'm not sure I'll be able to please him no matter what I do. I don't think I was ever what he wanted in a son, but after I lost my baseball scholarship, any confidence he had in me pretty much sank." He reached inside the basket and pulled out two pairs of binoculars. "But enough about that depressing subject. Here you go."

"Thanks. I like a man who's prepared."

He grinned and winked. "Then you're going to love me by the end of today."

Madison tried to suppress her smile—after all, she hadn't forgiven him quite yet—and turned her gaze back to the ocean. In the distance, a few surfers wove in and out of the waves in a lyrical choreography they seemed to know intimately. The sight mesmerized her and, somehow, lit a longing deep inside.

She lifted the binoculars to her eyes, first scanning the white-tipped waves close to the shore then the calmer waters farther out. "My aunt and I came here at least once a week during whale-watching season, more often if she could get away from her shop." It had been Chrissy's way of helping Madison to make peace with what had happened to her parents. After all, the migration pattern of whales was a constant, something she could rely on. And her aunt had been right there with her, always providing that place to come home to.

She'd been exactly what Madison had needed, but Madison hadn't returned the favor to Chrissy, had she? She should have occasionally come home. Should have checked in with her aunt more often.

"So you know what you're looking for, then? Because I ran out of time to research it, and if you don't know, we may just be staring at the waves all day."

Madison chuckled. "Yes, I know." She focused on a spot not too far away. "In fact, I think I've spotted our first whale group right now."

"No way. Seriously?"

"Mm-hmm." Yes, there was the familiar low plume of water. "There, see? It looks like a puff of smoke hovering just above the water. It's probably a pod of gray whales."

"I don't see it."

Madison glanced up at Evan, who was hunched forward squinting into his binoculars, a frown overtaking his lips. "Lift them a bit."

He did but overcorrected. She moved closer and adjusted them down just a hair. "It may take a minute to see them again. You probably won't see the actual whale. They don't breach the surface that often." Madison let her arm fall, but Evan caught her fingers in one hand while holding the binoculars steady with his other.

Her heart skipped at the contact.

Part of her itched to watch for the whales again, but a bigger part wanted to catch his reaction when he finally saw one for the first time. The frown remained on his face as he concentrated on watching, and the morning sunlight revealed blond scruff on his normally clean-shaven jaw. Madison breathed him in. He wasn't wearing his cologne today, but she was enjoying the natural smell of his soap and shampoo—the casual him—even more than the professional Evan.

Finally, his lips broke into a smile. "I saw it! There!"

Madison raised her binoculars and caught sight of the source of his exclamations. Not just one puff but several. "Hello, lovelies." Then one broke the surface, its gray-and-white-mottled body flitting out of the water for just a moment. "Did you see that?"

"And you said that didn't happen." He nudged her, a smile in his voice.

"I said it doesn't happen often. But sometimes, we get lucky." Aunt Chrissy used to say that whale watching was like life—completely unexpected. You never knew what you'd get, but you kept going, hoping to see something spectacular, to connect with nature, with God, in a new, profound way.

Evan squeezed Madison's hand, and the weight of his gaze upon her settled in her heart.

Madison put down the binoculars and turned to look at him.

He laced their fingers together and rubbed circles across the top of her hand. "That was incredible. How do you know so much about whales?"

"Aunt Chrissy and I checked out a bunch of books from the library and studied them together."

"Ah, and thus the librarian was born."

"Pretty sure I was born with a book in my hands."

"That would have been something to see."

She smiled. "Anyway, it kind of became the first thing we connected on. After my parents died, I pretty much shut down. It was hard for Chrissy—for anyone—to draw me out." It had taken a while for Madison to open up, make friends. But Chrissy never gave up on her.

"I can't even imagine what that must have been like. I mean, my parents aren't always my favorite people, but to lose them at such a young age . . ."

She sighed and found herself leaning against his side, watching the water undulate. He let go of her hand and wrapped his arm around her shoulders. "The sad truth of it is, I didn't really know my parents. Not all that well, anyway. They were gone a lot for work, always jetting off around the world. Leaving me behind with a nanny and a mountain of books."

"Books became your refuge."

"Yeah. And Aunt Chrissy, she saw that, how attached I was to them. She figured out a way to enter into my world and become part of it." Her chest squeezed. "I miss her."

"Me too." Evan's voice was low, almost reverent somehow, as it often was when he spoke about Aunt Chrissy.

He really had cared for her too, hadn't he? How could

Madison ever have accused him of anything less? "I've been wanting to ask—how did you and Aunt Chrissy get close, anyway?"

With a smile in his voice, he told her about how Aunt Chrissy had pulled him into doing some chores for her, then rewarded him with sweets, slowly breaking down his walls with conversation and sage wisdom. He credited her with helping him to turn over a new leaf, infusing him with confidence that real change was possible if he focused on what he wanted.

When he finished talking, Madison found herself smiling. "That sounds like something she'd do."

"What? Take in a stray in need of a second chance?" He chuckled.

"Well, you *do* have the most adorable puppy-dog eyes." Oh man, pour on the cheese, why didn't she? "What I mean is that she had the uncanny ability to see the hurt in others and do whatever it took to speak into their lives. I never would have become who I am today without her."

And yet, because Madison had acted so selfishly in staying away from Walker Beach, Aunt Chrissy had been without family in her final days.

Her hand trembled as she pushed away a few tears.

"Hey." Evan pulled back and looked into Madison's eyes. "What's wrong?"

"Nothing." An urge to lean into his arms again tugged at her. What was he doing to her resolve to stand on her own two feet? "I'm just realizing that I wasn't a good niece."

"That's not what Chrissy thought. She never stopped talking about you. That must be why I feel like I've known you all my life."

Except, he'd known her better than most—and not because of Chrissy. "You really don't remember, do you?" Or didn't know at all. Which was it?

His nose crinkled. "Remember what?"

"The letters."

"Letters?"

"Yeah. Senior year. The pen-pal program?"

His mouth pulled tightly. "What about it?"

She almost dropped it right then and there. If the past Evan *had* meant it all as a cruel joke, she almost didn't want to know anymore. But this Evan, he was different. She knew that now. Why would he fake all of this?

Yes, this guy . . . maybe he was worth trusting.

"Madison?" Her name drifted from his lips, caressing her cheeks before floating across the ocean on the wind.

She bit her lip as she looked at him. Swallowed hard. "I was your pen pal, Evan."

Yep, that was definitely surprise in his wide eyes. "What? How do you know?"

"Because I showed up that day we were going to meet. I saw it was you. And I thought . . ."

His hand lifted to tuck a strand of her hair behind her ear, but his eyes never left hers. "You thought what?"

"I—" Madison licked her lips. Man, this was harder than she'd thought it'd be. All those years of believing him to be one thing, when maybe she'd been wrong. "I was about to approach you when your friends came in. Roxy said something that made me think it was all a mean joke. So I ran. And when you tried following up with more letters, I couldn't fathom why someone would be so cruel. Why someone hated me so much."

"What? Really?" The anguish in his voice tore through her, and she wanted to kick the stupid, insecure girl she'd been. How different things might have turned out.

She broke eye contact with him, turning her head the other way as she pulled her knees into her chest. In the distance, but closer than before, puffs rose from the sea. Another pod of whales. The constant.

Breathing in deeply, Madison looked his way once more.

"I'm sorry, Evan. It's just, after the way your friends treated me and the way you . . ."

"The way I let them." His lips twisted into a grimace. "You have nothing to be sorry for, Madison. I was a complete waste of space back then. Half the time, I was drunk, so I don't have much more than hazy memories of most of those years. But I do know that my pen pal—you—were the one person I was honest with, about everything. And when you didn't show up, I thought . . . well, actually, what I thought turned out to be accurate."

"Which was what?" Without thinking, she reached up, cupping his cheek, aching to soothe the pain clear on his face.

He shrugged. "That my pen pal saw it was me and decided I wasn't worth her time after all." Though he tried to crack a smile, she saw past it to the hurting teen he'd been.

To the man who still wondered if he was good enough. Worth fighting for.

Worth staying for.

She hated that she'd hurt him. That he'd hurt her. That they'd hurt each other. But maybe it wasn't too late to heal the wounds of those hurts, to try again. To rebuild.

"We aren't the same people we were back then, Evan." Madison snuggled into him again, relaxing her cheek against the soft fabric of his sweater as the ocean danced below. "I'm choosing to believe that, and I hope you can too."

CHAPTER 8

The promotion was slipping through Evan's fingers faster than Javier Baez stealing home.

According to his buddy in HR, a flood of applications for Denise's replacement had come in—some of them outside hires who were extremely well-qualified. But Evan had a plan. He only hoped it would be enough to convince the city council to give him a chance.

Taking a deep breath, Evan pushed open the door of City Hall's conference room. Most of the city council members were there already. Bud Travis, lounging in his worn green windbreaker, nodded as Evan entered. The antique-store owner Kiki Baker West chatted amiably with Doug Doyle, a slick forty-something realtor who owned several of the buildings downtown. Travel agent Rosa Diaz had already informed Evan she would be out of town and couldn't make the last-minute meeting, which just left—

"I sure would like to know what this meeting is about, son." Evan's father breezed through the door, dressed in a three-piece suit despite the fact it was casual Friday. "And why it had to happen ASAP." He quirked an eyebrow and slid into his self-designated seat at the head of the table.

Evan closed the door behind him. "Thank you all for coming on such short notice. I know you're busy and have a lot going on, and that meeting on a Friday afternoon is probably the last thing you feel like doing, so I'll make this as quick and painless as possible."

He moved to the front of the room and felt four pairs of eyes on him as he turned on the projector hooked up to his laptop. "As you are aware, Hole-in-the-Wall Hardware is set to reopen soon, which means the agreement with Herman Hardware is no longer on the table." The screen behind him flickered on, revealing a presentation with a blank first page.

His dad's frown was pronounced, while Bud Travis's grin didn't hide his glee over the turn of events. The other two just nodded.

Evan continued. "They aren't the first chain to consider opening a location here, but they're certainly the largest. It's no secret that our projections showed how they'd have been a boon to the economy—and quickly—but we'd still need several similar deals to help things get back to where they were before the earthquake. Which got me thinking."

His finger hovered over the button that would bring up the first slide, and he swallowed his nerves. He'd met with Alex several times this week to check and recheck the numbers, so he trusted the truth behind what he was saying. And while he'd spent much of his free time in the evenings helping Madison ready her store for the grand reopening tomorrow, Evan had gone down the rabbit hole with this idea during work hours, diving deeply so he understood all the implications and potential pitfalls.

"In light of this, and with a desire not to rely on outside forces so much to get our tourism and economy back on track,

I've been considering some other options. There are grants, et cetera, and if we win them, they'd have a cumulative effect. But I want us to think bigger." Evan flipped to the next slide: *The Christmas on the Beach Festival.*

"A festival?" Kiki's voice perked up.

"Yes. One with live music, food, games, a tree lighting ceremony, and fireworks over the water." He'd been sitting there on the rocks whale watching with Madison last weekend, holding her, soaking in her warmth against him—still reeling from the news that she'd been the pen pal who had made him feel so accepted all those years ago—when he'd allowed his gaze to wander down toward the sandy beach. Baker Park was acres big, and the community developer in him asked why the town had never held a festival there. "I'm not going to lie. It would take a lot of work, and the entire community would need to get on board with it. Businesses would need to contribute services and products, and we'd have to gather a committee to organize it. But I think it's something people could really get behind."

He waited a beat, assuming there would be questions, but silence greeted him. All right, then.

Evan used the presentation clicker to move to the next slide. "Other towns similar to ours have benefitted greatly from festivals like the one I'm proposing. Yes, they had more time to plan them, but we have ten and a half months. I've already spoken with local events coordinator Ashley Baker, and she was excited about it. She believes that if everyone rallies behind the idea and pitches in, this town could create a very lucrative event that would provide a lot of extra funds to disperse throughout the community and shore up our economy."

"This all sounds well and good, son, but we already have our sesquicentennial celebration in December. We don't want to overshadow that."

"That's exactly right, Mayor. We don't want to overshadow it. We want to make it bigger and better."

The second the words left his lips, he had to fight the cringe that was a natural reaction whenever he said something he knew his father wouldn't like. The sesquicentennial celebration had been another of his father's pet projects, and Evan had no doubt Dad had almost been looking at it as a victory party once he was re-elected in the fall.

"Pardon my ignorance." Raising his hand, Bud spoke up from the back of the room. "But could you explain how you'd get a profit out of this? Events like the one you're describing—all the food, the rentals, the marketing, the entertainment—seem like they'd be mighty expensive."

"Great point, Bud," his father butted in. "I'd think several smaller wins, like the deal with Herman Hardware, would be less risky and consume far fewer resources."

Evan tried to ignore how his dad's eyes bore into him. "First of all, I have a contact who's assured me we could get a grant for a decent chunk of the costs to the city. And, sure, it would take a lot more coordination and effort, but I think it would allow the people of this town a chance to contribute, to feel part of something. That's where the true strength of a community is found—not in the economy, which fluctuates, but in its spirit."

"I'm not convinced."

Evan fought for control over his facial expressions and forced civility into his voice. "About what, Mayor Walsh?"

"We need to show people that we are taking care of this for them. They need to have confidence in us. Quicker wins will lead to more confidence, which will lead to less panic should the economy worsen. This is especially important with our big tourism season coming up in the summer."

Translation: He wanted to give the people a reason to vote for him again.

Politics was the worst part of this job. And if Evan snagged the head community developer position, he'd have to endure even more of it.

Flexing his jaw, he searched for a response that would not reveal his true emotions.

"What I want to know is, why not both?" Doug hit the edge of the table with a fancy fountain pen, seemingly unaware of how he'd temporarily rescued Evan. "I don't really see a downside to the festival, so long as we have a way to fund it, and it sounds like we do. But why don't we also keep pursuing opportunities like the one with Herman Hardware?"

"We definitely will. That's in my job description, after all. I was more thinking about a larger-scale attempt that would not require us to rely on one person or one deal." And that would give him a leg up over the other job applicants. "To answer your earlier questions, Bud, we could use several tactics to raise funds. Corporate sponsorships, ticket sales, raffles, a silent auction. We could also ask each of the food vendors to pay a fee for a spot or donate a portion of their sales back to the town. There'd be a lot of banding together and individual contributions from our local business owners and townspeople. But I think Walker Beach is up for the challenge, don't you?"

Bud's eyes sparkled. "I do, young man. Indeed, I do."

"Great." He answered a few more questions then checked his watch. "Sorry, I kept you all longer than intended. Before you go, though, I'd like to hear your thoughts about adding this to the city council meeting agenda next week."

"I think it's a great idea." Bud flashed him a thumbs-up and winked. "We just need to let the public know that we'll be discussing something they'll be interested in weighing in on."

Gathering her belongings, Kiki stood. "I need to run, but I second that. Fabulous idea, Evan."

Doug nodded. "I'll make sure it gets added as an item to present and discuss with the town. We can gauge their reaction and go from there. Sounds like we'd want to move on it quickly if we decide to move forward."

"Absolutely." Evan couldn't stop grinning. What had started as a way to secure himself a promotion had actually blossomed into something he could see having a true widespread effect on the town for the better.

And the look of respect in the council members' eyes? He'd take that too.

As the others filtered out, Evan turned to the projector and unplugged his computer.

"That girl's really gotten to you, hasn't she?"

Yanking the power cord from the wall, Evan bundled it into his hands and faced his father. "What?"

The mayor folded his arms across his burly chest and stared down at Evan. Never had Dad's two extra inches seemed so tall. "I thought you'd be able to work on her, but clearly the opposite is true. You haven't changed one bit, have you? Always letting those of the female persuasion affect your judgment—first Miss Chamberlain, now this Price girl."

OK, so they were going there, were they? "I don't know how many times I have to tell you this. But my decision to drink that night in high school had nothing to do with impressing Roxy. I was just . . . it doesn't matter why I did it. I screwed up, and I paid for it." In more ways than just losing his college scholarship. "But this is completely different. Madison is different."

So different. His dad didn't even know the half of it. Evan was only beginning to scratch the surface when it came to what he felt for her, how he was different in her presence than in anyone else's. Because, for the first time—well, the first time since Chrissy—he could just be himself. No pretending. No impressing. Now that they'd cleared up misunderstandings over their pasts, he knew without a doubt that Madison respected him. Liked him for him. He didn't have to do anything to earn that respect. She offered it freely.

And he wasn't going to do anything to screw that up.

"Yet you still haven't convinced her to close the hardware store."

"No." To be honest, he hadn't tried, but he didn't have the energy at the moment to get into that.

The air between them crackled as Evan waited, fists clenched, for more judgment to come his way.

Instead, his dad grunted, turned, and left.

So now Evan wasn't even worth a response? Figured. He'd finally done something he was proud of and it wasn't enough. In fact, it was the exact opposite of what his dad wanted from him.

Evan snagged his laptop and headed back to his office.

Madison stood there, hands behind her back, teeth tugging at her bottom lip.

He halted. "Hey."

"Hey, yourself." She stepped forward as if to hug him then stopped. "I was hoping you were free tonight."

He'd planned to grab take out and go over the details of the proposed festival one more time. But now that she was here? No way. "I'm all yours."

~

"I'm all yours."

Evan hadn't meant his words the way Madison was taking them, yet she couldn't help feeling warm despite the cool Friday night air that hit as she climbed from the cab of his truck. She'd directed him first to the Frosted Cake to pick up an order, and then about five minutes away, up into the residential area that hugged the hills. Trees surrounded them on all sides except for the open space before them, where a park was nestled inside the neighborhood. Clouds gathered on the horizon, threatening her plans, but she prayed they'd hold off the rain until she'd accomplished what she came here to do.

"So are we planning to swing and hit the slides?" Evan joined Madison on her side of the vehicle, the food bag in hand.

She hoisted a large duffel bag from the back of the truck. "Nope."

"When did you stick that in there?"

"Before I came to snag you from your office." They started off toward the picnic tables. Surprisingly, the park was almost deserted, with just an older man and woman walking their dog in the distance. Perhaps the chilly evening weather was keeping others away, or maybe they simply had more happening places to be on their first night of the weekend. Whatever the case, Madison didn't mind the alone time with Evan.

"You were so sure I'd say yes, huh?" He bumped her as they walked.

A smile tugged at her lips. "When a woman offers a man food, there's a pretty good chance he'll take her up on it." Not that she'd cooked. She hadn't had time, what with the grand reopening tomorrow. But after working hard all week—with Evan and Ashley pitching in when they could—she'd done everything possible to be ready.

"The food smells great, don't get me wrong, but the company's not bad either."

They arrived at two picnic tables underneath a blue ramada. "You're right." Madison set the duffel onto the ground and slid onto a bench. "The food does smell great."

"Ha ha." He put the food bag on the table and sat across from her, granting her an easy excuse to watch him. Even in his casual wear, he was easy on the eyes. Tonight, his hair curled slightly over the collar of his long-sleeved T-shirt. Normally, he kept his hair neat and tidy, but he'd been so busy helping her this week, he hadn't even taken time to shave. Madison found she preferred the rugged and scruffy look on him.

The buttoned-up guy was the one he wanted everyone else

to see. She liked thinking that he was willing to show her a different side of himself.

"Do I have something on my face?" His lips twisted into a wry smile.

"Sorry." She turned her attention back to their food, rustling in the bag to pull out two containers.

"I don't mind."

Goodness, if the tips of one's ears could blush, she had a feeling hers were. Madison cleared her throat and pushed Evan's still-warm food container toward him as thunder rumbled in the distance.

He peeked inside and whistled. "Meatloaf and potatoes. You really do know the way to a man's heart."

"You're not that hard to please." She'd meant the comment flippantly, teasingly, but something twisted unexpectedly in the pit of her stomach as she popped open the lid to her chef salad.

Because despite all Evan had done for her, she couldn't help but wonder whether he was being so nice because he had cared about Chrissy and, therefore, Madison as an extension.

Or was there more to it for him?

Since that time he'd brought pizza, there hadn't been any moments when she thought he might kiss her again, not even on their "date" to watch the whales when she'd snuggled next to him and practically willed him to with her mind. But she should be OK with that. After all, they had a history, even if he didn't remember it. Maybe it was best to let bygones be bygones, to embrace an unexpected friendship—a kinship with someone else who had loved Aunt Chrissy—and be satisfied with that.

Tonight wasn't about figuring out what was between them. It was about thanking Evan for all he'd done to help her. She didn't need anything from him. He'd given enough already.

"Shall we? Then we can get to the really fun part." She handed him a fork and started eating her salad.

"What exactly do you have planned?" Evan tucked into his

meatloaf and groaned. "Whatever it is, the answer is yes. You're my hero right about now."

"That's only fair, since you've been mine the last few weeks."

He paused, lifting an eyebrow.

"I would never have gotten the store ready for reopening if it weren't for you. Thank you, from the bottom of my heart."

Evan studied her for a moment, his Adam's apple bobbing. Then, he nodded. "Yeah, of course. No big deal." He shoved another bite of potatoes into his mouth.

"Don't discount it. It's a huge deal." She pushed a chunk of bacon around on the top of her salad. "You have a life, a job. Yet you've spent countless hours helping me, a stranger."

"You're not a stranger, Mad."

Mad. Something about the way he said the nickname—that he'd used a nickname at all—sent a tingle up her spine. "Well, I was, and you still helped me. So tonight is my way of thanking you."

"I have to admit something to you." He winced. "Originally, my motives for helping you weren't so pure."

"What do you mean?"

"You know that promotion I've mentioned?"

"You mean the one you're going to snag after you get the whole town on board with the Christmas festival?"

His laugh came out short, a bit disbelieving. "Yeah. Well, anyway, that's part of the reason I was fighting so hard for Herman Hardware in the first place. I thought it would help me stand out among the applicants. And when I found out Herman wasn't happening, I figured helping you get your store open would look good on my resume."

That answered that question, then. Not that she could blame him. The man had lost the Herman opportunity because of her.

Madison stabbed a tomato. "I understand." And she did, however disappointing it was to hear.

"But." He slid his hand across the table, and with a tentative movement she gave him hers. He rubbed her fingers with a light touch of the tip of his thumb. "That changed pretty much after that first night of helping you. By then, I was hooked. I just wanted to spend more time with you."

She burst out laughing. A flash of hurt crossed his face, and Madison rushed to explain. "I was the one who was hooked, remember? Quite literally, in fact."

"You know, when we met, you weren't exactly the joking type." He grinned. "Looks like I'm rubbing off on you."

"Maybe you are." After a moment, she grew sober, inhaling. "Thanks for telling me that, Evan. You didn't have to."

"I wanted to be honest. But I'm serious about it becoming about more than a job to me. It's been an absolute pleasure to help you." He cocked his head. "How are you feeling about tomorrow?"

The sun had set and the park, ramada, and fields beyond were bathed in inviting light that spilled from the streetlamps and floodlights spread throughout the public space. "All the things. Nervous. Excited. Really, really hoping I don't fail."

"You won't."

"How can you be so sure?"

"Because I know you." The words soaked into the dry and thirsty places of her heart, the ones she'd deprived of water for so long. "And you can do anything you set your mind to, Madison Price. Of that I'm sure."

"Thank you, Evan. I believe the same about you."

His staccato laugh proved he didn't believe what she was saying.

Madison threaded her fingers through his and fixed him with a pseudo-stern look. "I mean it. Look at how you've turned your life around. Chrissy believed in you and so do I."

And she did. The thought comforted and scared the living daylights out of her.

His eyes followed the contours of her face, landing on her lips, and for a few heartbeats of a moment—one, two—she waited breathlessly for him to cross to her side of the table, to feed the connection she felt between them.

But instead, he looked away, as if studying the long grains of the wooden table. "So, what's this fun part of our night you keep alluding to?" The tease in his voice sounded forced.

Madison pushed past the disappointment in her heart. "Are you done eating?"

"Yeah." He polished off the last bite of his meatloaf and stood. "Let's do this . . . whatever *this* is."

"Go ahead and look in that bag, then."

He squatted and unzipped the duffel then pulled the sides open to reveal the baseball equipment inside. "Seriously? You play?"

"No." Ben Baker had been gracious enough to loan her the bag. "But you do." And she'd wanted to see him in his element—his true element, not the one he'd invented so others would respect him.

"I *used* to play. There's a difference." His shoulders slumped as he re-zipped the bag then stood and walked to the edge of the ramada.

She joined him. "It's still a part of you." Slipping her hand into his once more, she leaned against him. "And I, for one, want to see that part come out and play. So, come on."

Madison tugged him toward the bag, which he reluctantly grabbed and hoisted onto his shoulder. Together, they trudged to the well-lit baseball field and got out gloves, a ball, and a bat. A raindrop splatted against Madison's cheek as she tossed the ball to Evan.

Despite the fact it went high, he jumped and caught it with ease. For a moment, he stood on the pitcher's mound, his glove in one hand, ball cradled in the other. "I haven't played since I lost my scholarship, you know." He sent the ball sailing back to Madison.

It came right to her, but it fell between her willing hands. "I didn't know that. If you'd rather not . . ."

"No, it's OK."

They tossed the ball back and forth in silence, Madison fielding most of the ones he sent her thanks to her inability to catch them. More rain sprinkled from the sky but not enough to chill her, so they kept playing.

Evan hit some balls across the field with the bat, and Madison chased them, laughing at how ridiculous she felt. She had a feeling that the returning grin on Evan's face meant he was laughing at her too.

She jogged back and deposited the ball into his waiting hand. The whole field smelled of good, clean earth thanks to the rain.

"You want to take a turn batting?"

To tell the truth, she'd started to shiver a bit but wasn't ready to leave. Here, Evan was so full of life, so . . . himself. The confidence he exuded on the field, holding a bat like a sword, was deliciously appealing.

Aaaand, yep, she'd read one too many romance novels.

Madison cleared her throat. "Um, sure." She took the offered bat and attempted to stand the way he had—elbows out, rear extended, head cocked. Did she look as dumb as she felt?

"Want some help?"

"Please."

The rain started falling harder, hitting the dirt with force, but Madison couldn't move a muscle once Evan was near, guiding her hands. He hesitated then eased closer. "Do you mind?" The husky question rumbled in his throat.

"Please." The irony of her repeated answer couldn't have escaped him, but he didn't say a word, just placed his arms around hers as he positioned them into the right slant. Then his hands crept to her hips, maneuvering her into a much more natural angle.

But instead of moving away, he stayed there, holding her arms from behind her, cradling her against the sudden onslaught of rain. It would be impossible for her to hear his heart beating over the drum of the water slapping the earth. But it seemed like she could.

Then again, maybe that was her own.

"Madison." One word whispered in her ear, but it was filled with such emotion that she glanced back at him. Rain clouded her vision, keeping her from fully seeing him, but his face was close enough that the warmth of his breath on her cheek sent her heart into a rapid beat. Dropping the bat at their feet, she slowly straightened and turned—right into his embrace—then lifted her hands and traced his cheeks with her fingers.

He leaned into her touch, and as her hand passed over his mouth, he kissed her palm. Slowly, he dragged his lips along the edge of her hand until he reached the tips of her fingers.

Madison inhaled, relishing the feel of his lips against her skin. Her entire body shook—from the cold or the flood of emotion or the pounding of the rain in her ears, who could tell? —but she reveled in this feeling of being alive, of being wanted, of allowing someone close.

And still, Evan didn't kiss her mouth the way her body ached for him to. But she could feel him looking at her, and it was a caress, a longing, matching her desire.

So why . . .

Maybe he was waiting for her to make the first move. Could she do that?

Yes.

The word wound itself around her heart and tugged upward, toward Evan. So Madison moved her hands around the back of his neck, playing with the tuft of hair she'd noticed earlier, then drew his head down.

He didn't resist, and his mouth overtook hers.

For a moment, she simply allowed the water from the heavens to course down her face, giving in to the pleasure of his lips pressing against her own, of their bodies held together, their arms interwoven. Then, his kiss became more urgent, and he grabbed the sides of her sweatshirt, pulling her even closer.

Madison could feel the muscles beneath his shirt as her hands drifted down from his neck, to his chest, to his shoulders, exploring their connection, embracing what this could mean, trying not to think, just to feel.

And oh, how good it felt.

Finally, they pulled away, both breathless. Evan placed his forehead against hers. "Wow. That was . . . incredible. Though I shouldn't be surprised."

"And why is that?"

"Because you rock at everything you do." He snagged the baseball equipment and led her toward the ramada, out of the rain. Once he'd set down the bag, he leaned back against the picnic table and tucked her against him.

She wound her arms around the trunk of his solid body and put her head against his chest. "Thanks, but the reality is there's one thing I may very well fail at."

"I doubt it."

Now that the nerves over the evening had passed, her mind was released to think once again about the store opening in the morning. "Guess we'll see tomorrow." The rain beat against the ramada roof, like a drummer given free rein during a solo.

He pulled back, lifting her chin to look her in the eyes. "I don't need to see. I know you'll make Chrissy proud."

His words were sweet, but Madison saw all the ways she lacked the necessary knowledge. There simply hadn't been time to learn it all.

Evan's eyes probed. "You look like you could use a distraction." A sudden smile curled around his lips.

Despite herself, Madison grinned as well. “Did you have anything in mind?”

He bent toward her, touching her nose to his. “I’m sure I could think of something.” His lips flirted with hers as he spoke.

“Please enlighten me.”

“With pleasure.” And he did.

CHAPTER 9

Every day Madison Price impressed him more and more.

Today was no exception.

With his free hand, Evan pushed his way through the front door of Hole-in-the-Wall Hardware, and a bell overhead announced his arrival. Inside, townspeople milled about the brightened space, some carrying items for purchase, others chatting in the aisles about how their weekend was going.

And there was Madison, helping old Dottie Wildman select paint colors from her collection. Surrounded by organized buckets of nails, screws, and washers, the wall of color swatches and paint cans livened up the corner of the store.

At his approach, Madison glanced up, and a huge smile lit her face. Was she remembering last night? He hadn't been able to get their kiss—kisses—out of his mind. "Hey." Her eyes flew to the box in his hand, and, if possible, her grin widened. "Are those what I think they are?"

Dottie turned, squinting. "What did you bring us, young man?"

He opened the flap of the box. "A dozen donuts from the Frosted Cake."

"My hero. I didn't eat breakfast." Madison motioned for Dottie to take one.

The older woman waved her hand at the box. "No, no, that would ruin my blood sugar for the day. But you go ahead, dear. I think I'm going to take this swatch home and ask Mr. Wildman which he prefers for the bathroom. It's so good to see you again. I always knew you'd make something of yourself." The retired librarian patted Madison on the cheek.

Were those tears shining in Madison's eyes? "Thank you. It's wonderful to see you as well."

Dottie shuffled off, clutching a swatch with an array of bright orange colors.

Evan leaned in. "Do you think there's something wrong with her vision? Those paint colors are something else."

Madison sniffled and laughed while her fingers hovered over the box. "I tried to steer her more toward the calming blues, but she insisted that orange is her husband's favorite color." Snagging a chocolate long john, she took a bite and groaned. "Oh man. That's amazing." The donut left behind a smudge of chocolate at the corner of her mouth.

Evan itched to swoop in and kiss it away. But he didn't want to presume, so he reached up slowly with his thumb and rubbed it off. "Your donut left a mark."

"Oh. Thanks."

"I'd better let you get back to work." He closed the box as he glanced around. Even more customers flowed into the store. "How's it going?"

They started walking toward the front desk where the owner of the local plant nursery waited with a hammer in his hand. "Great so far. I mean, I've only been open for about an hour, but I've had a lot of traffic just in that time. May have something to do with the raffle I'm holding—winner gets a fifty-dollar gift card—but I figured if I can just get people in the door, I've made progress."

"I doubt it's the raffle. Everyone's been waiting on pins and needles for a hardware store they don't have to drive a half-hour to."

While she rang up Ned, Evan placed the donuts in the back on the little table in the break room. He chose a strawberry donut with sprinkles for himself and polished it off in three bites before returning to the main part of the store.

Already, Madison was showing hippie artist Jules Baker—Chrissy's best friend and the owner of Serene Art next door—the display of tools on the other side of the store. Although Evan couldn't hear what she was saying, the confidence in Madison's tone drifted across the space as she pointed to various tools. Her posture indicated the same ease, as did her laughter. And when Jules leaned in to give Madison a long hug, Madison squeezed back with fervor.

On her way from talking with Jules, Madison caught him staring at her. "What?" The flash of vulnerability in her eyes did something to his insides, made Evan want to pull her to him and reassure her of what he was feeling.

Don't screw it up.

He batted away the thought and smiled. "Just proud of you, that's all. The town is really rallying to support you. You're doing it."

As she maneuvered around him to the spot behind the counter, he allowed his hands to skim her waist, and her eyes snapped to his, holding his gaze for what seemed like hours, not seconds. Finally, she spoke. "It wouldn't have been possible without your help."

"Nah, I was just the brawn. You're the brains behind all of this. And the heart too."

"Chrissy was—is—the heart."

If he hadn't known her like he did, he'd have missed the slight tremble in Madison's lips. He joined her behind the counter and snagged her hand, squeezing it. "You both are."

"I feel her here, you know? And . . . I hope she'd be proud. I didn't let the family legacy die."

Evan cocked his head to the side, studying her. "It's not the store she cared about. It was you."

"I know. But still. I feel like she'd approve, you know?"

Would she have approved of her niece giving up her dream of being a librarian to run the family store? It was impossible to know, but Evan *was* sure of one thing. "She'd have supported you doing whatever you wanted to do."

Madison's eyes narrowed slightly. Frowning, she fiddled with the keys of the cash register. "So, you think this was a mistake?"

"That's not what I said at all." Great, he'd stepped in it. "I just meant that Chrissy was the kind to support the people she loved in following their dreams. And I support you too."

A teenage boy called to Madison for some help, and she turned a tight smile to Evan. "I've got to go."

"Want me to man the register?"

"I don't need you to."

"But can I? I'd love to help somehow."

Madison placed her hand on his arm. "You've already done more than I could ever repay."

"I can think of a way for you to repay me."

And there it was—that shy smile that somehow captivated him more than a flirtatious one ever could. "We will have to see about that, Mr. Walsh." Then she headed off to help her customer, and Evan stayed put in case someone needed to check out while she was away.

The bell sounded over the door, and Evan stifled a groan

when Roxy sauntered in. What was she doing in town? Maybe she was just visiting her folks, but her roving eyes gave her a calculated appearance. She beelined for him. "So, my sources were right."

"Hey, Roxy." *Just ignore her and don't cause a scene.* "How can we help you?"

"We? Now, that's just the most adorable thing." She tucked a soft tendril of hair behind her ear. "I'm surprised at you, Evan Walsh. First you play the girl, making her think you weren't plotting against her store the entire time you were, well, whatever you were doing with her. And now you're here working or being supportive or whatever, even though you know what's coming."

"What are you talking about?"

She rolled her eyes. "As if you don't know." But after a few major beats of silence, she leaned on the counter with one hand. "Wait. You don't know?"

"Know what?"

"Oh, that's funny. Well, I don't want to be the one to spoil the surprise." As she turned to leave, Roxy's heel scraped the wood floor.

Evan moved around the desk and snagged her elbow. He prayed Madison wouldn't see him talking to Roxy, who seemed to be a sore subject. "Stop."

Roxy's small glittering eyes laughed at him. "Yes?"

He led her toward the aisle by the door, where Madison wouldn't see them. "What do you know?"

"Just that it's a shame that Madison's gone to all this work to open a store that's going to be forced to close soon anyway." Despite her words, her tone conveyed pleasure in the sentiment.

Why did Roxy always feel the need to cause trouble? But the real question was whether her information was true or made up for drama's sake. "OK, I'll bite. Who's going to force Madison out of business?"

"Who do you think?"

"Aldrin?" At her conspiratorial smile, he shook his head. "No, he's not interested in opening a location here since a viable hardware store is in place."

"Maybe he's reconsidered." She was enjoying this way too much, drawing the conversation out on purpose. "I won't say any more right now except that Madison Price shouldn't get too comfortable here."

Waiting for a middle-aged couple to walk by, Evan crossed his arms over his chest and lowered his voice. "I'm the assistant community developer. This was my deal from the start. I would know what you're talking about if your words had any truth to them."

"OK, Evan. Sure." Roxy smirked then moved her gaze to the left. "Oh, hi, Madison. Great job on the store."

Evan swung around to find Madison ten steps away. Confusion filled her gaze. "Uh, thanks."

"Gotta go. Can't wait to hear how things go for you." Roxy blew a kiss and left.

Evan joined Madison. "Once again, it's not what it looks like."

She bit her lip then nodded. "OK."

"OK?"

"Yeah, OK. I trust you, Evan."

And with her words, something expanded inside his chest. She believed him. Believed in him, if her words last night on the baseball field were any indication.

He believed in her too—in her ability to start what she finished, to do something that she felt unprepared for, to stand up for what she believed in. And that inspired him.

As he pulled Madison into a hug and kissed the top of her head, he couldn't help worrying. What if Roxy hadn't been bluffing? What would that do to Madison? And if the hardware store really were threatened, what would *Madison* do?

Would she stay and fight? Or would she go on with her life—move away from here—to become the person she'd intended to be before she'd returned to Walker Beach?

CHAPTER 10

Until now, Madison had managed to avoid city council meetings for the most part.

So she'd had no idea that just about the entire town showed up to these things. Or maybe it was just tonight since Evan's festival was on the agenda. Her eyes scanned City Hall's council chambers, where nearly every seat was filled five minutes before the meeting began. Apparently, this was the place to be.

Beside her, Evan pointed to a few open spots down front with Reserved signs attached. "Come on. Those are our seats."

She had to lean in to hear over the din of chatter. "I don't have to sit so close."

"But I'm presenting, and you're with me." Snagging her hand in his, Evan winked.

Madison pinched him on the wrist.

"Ow. What was that for?"

"Just checking that you're real. That this is all real." Because, seriously, there were so many times when it didn't feel like it. That she was back in Walker Beach, for one. And that she was dating Evan Walsh. Not that they'd said as much. But she didn't just go around kissing random people unless it meant something. She prayed the same was true for him.

Evan lifted his eyebrows, grinning. "You know you're supposed to pinch yourself, not some poor unsuspecting guy."

"That's not how I remember it."

Laughing, he led her through the crowd, maneuvering her with ease past fellow town residents. A middle-aged woman with big red hair tied back in a bandanna talked with a group of Stepford-esque mavens in a loud, animated voice.

Evan leaned in close. "Be careful of that one. She moved here about eight years ago, but you'd think she was a lifer the way she knows everything about everyone. Name's Carlotta Jenkins."

She lifted her eyebrows. "The queen of the gossips?" Ashley had mentioned her.

"That's the one."

In another circle, businessmen in suits discussed something in hushed tones. A pack of young college-aged students laughed as they watched something on one of their phones.

Evan pointed out a group of tall thirty-somethings with a clear family resemblance to one another. Most of their clothing was nondescript, but one of the guys wore scrubs and one of the women sported a dark blue Walker Beach Fire Department T-shirt. "You remember the Griffin sextuplets? Most of them still live here. They're Ashley's cousins."

Madison swallowed, shook her head. There were still so many faces she didn't know.

Of course, knowing who people were didn't make someone part of a town. That much had been proven when she'd lived here the first time.

But as she and Evan made their way to their seats, people yelled hello to them. Always comfortable in a crowd, Evan returned the greetings with a smile and a shout as he pulled her along. He also introduced her to his office mate and friend, Alex, who she vaguely remembered from school.

They arrived at their seats, and she slid into the second one from the outside, allowing Evan the seat on the aisle so he could exit easily when it came time for him to present his idea for the festival.

When Madison heard her name, she turned to find Ben Baker and his girlfriend Bella behind her. They'd come into the store yesterday seeking wood, paint, and other supplies for some remodeling projects around the inn. Bella had told Madison a bit of her and Ben's story and it was interesting—and sigh-worthy—to say the least.

She glanced down the aisle and saw Mrs. Wildman sharing some popcorn out of a Ziploc bag with her husband Bill. Madison usually reserved the salty snack for the movie theater. Perhaps Mrs. Wildman expected a show here tonight.

She grinned at the thought.

As if sensing her attention, Mrs. Wildman looked up and waved.

"Seems you have a fan." Evan's voice caught her ear, and she turned to find him close, his eyes lit with amusement.

"She always was the sweetest lady." It had been so nice reconnecting with her Saturday at the store.

"I ran into her this morning at the Frosted Cake—"

"You were there again?"

"Not a word, woman." Evan bumped her shoulder with his own. "She couldn't sing your praises enough. In fact, several people I've talked to since Saturday were complimentary of you and the store."

"Really?" Without warning, Madison's eyes burned. The grand reopening had been more of a success than she'd dared hope for on such short notice. At first she'd felt awkward chatting about hammers and screws and all things DIY—she was no expert, despite reading more than ten books on the subject. But hour by hour, things had shifted, and she'd allowed herself to channel Aunt Chrissy, remembering how she'd been with customers. Madison had mimicked her memories of her aunt, and from then on, the day had gone smoothly.

"Really." Evan looked like he wanted to say more, but at that moment, his father called the meeting to order, and Evan straightened, his face wiped of any humor.

Madison squeezed his hand and moved her attention to the mayor, who sat in the middle at a semi-round table on a dais. The four city council members flanked him on either side. Bud caught her eye and winked.

"Welcome to our meeting, folks," Mayor Walsh said into the microphone affixed to the table in front of him. "Thank you for joining us. We have a full agenda, so we're going to dive right in."

For fifteen or so minutes they recapped agenda items from the last meeting and what they'd done to advance or kill those initiatives. Then, the mayor invited Ashley Baker up to the podium to discuss the latest developments with the library board.

Madison had meant to call Ashley to arrange a time to help her with the library project. She'd just gotten so backlogged with reopening Aunt Chrissy's store that she hadn't had time. But now, there were no excuses. She'd call her friend tomorrow—or better yet, grab her after the meeting tonight and find a time to lend a hand. A town needed a library, and if Madison could do anything to help, she would.

Ashley walked up to the podium, which faced the council members, and thanked the mayor. "As you know, we've been meeting to discuss a new location for the library, given that the state of the current property is in such disrepair. I won't bore you with the details, but let's just say that mold and books don't mix well."

A collective murmur spread through the crowd. Madison's

heart ached at the thought of so many ruined books. And her ruined sanctuary.

"The trouble is, there are no viable properties on Main Street that aren't currently spoken for."

That wasn't true. Two storefronts stood open right next to Hole-in-the-Wall Hardware. But maybe their leases were being negotiated by some new businesses. Madison turned to Evan to ask him what he knew, but he'd scooted forward to the edge of his seat, his forehead furrowed.

"So for now, we are still searching for the right place. We will also be using the insurance funds left to us to order new materials, but if you have any donations, please drop them off at Charmed, I'm Sure Books. Samantha Griffin has graciously agreed to collect for us. And while you're there, you can purchase some new reading material."

Ashley's hands rustled the paper she held as she discussed a few more updates, like the fact she'd commissioned the council for a salary to hire a head librarian. "Dottie Wildman has decided to retire, and as most of you know, she was a volunteer. But we'd like to take our reopened library to a whole new level, and we feel that requires paying a full-time employee or two."

Madison felt Evan's eyes on her and turned her head. "What?" she whispered.

"That sounds right up your alley."

"In case you haven't noticed, I have a job." She shot him a wry smile.

He didn't smile back. In fact, he frowned.

OK, then.

"Before I hand it back to Mayor Walsh, does anyone have any questions?"

"I do." A woman Madison didn't recognize stood. Someone rushed to hand her a microphone. "Why can't the library go in the spot between the hardware store and the golf course? Two open storefronts are available."

Before Ashley could answer, the mayor waved his hand in the air. "We have a potential new store going in there—one that will bring lots of jobs to Walker Beach—but that is still under discussion, so I can't say any more."

At that, Evan gripped Madison's hand painfully hard. What was going on with him?

"Thank you for the updates, Ms. Baker." The mayor cleared his throat. "And now we will move on to the reason most of you are probably here. I'd like to welcome to the stage our assistant community development officer, Evan Walsh, who is going to present our idea for preventing the economic disaster that may overcome Walker Beach if we aren't proactive."

Poor Evan. He'd lost plenty of sleep working out the details, and his dad hadn't supported the idea at all. Now, it was being presented as his idea too. At times like this, she wished he'd stand up to the mayor.

"Go." Madison nudged Evan toward the stage. "Save our town."

With a ghost of a smile, he stood and approached the podium.

And it took Madison a full minute before she realized she'd called it "our" town without flinching. Without hesitation. For the first time in forever, the idea of calling Walker Beach home felt right.

~

He should have been ecstatic. The presentation had gone off without a hitch, and the townspeople had been fully supportive and enthusiastic about the idea for a festival despite the amount of work it would take to pull off. And the icing on the cake—the council had unanimously approved it.

But all he felt was a cool ball of rage growing in his gut.

Evan tried to be polite as town residents stopped him on his way out of the auditorium, patting him on the back and exclaiming that his "great idea" was going to save Walker Beach —not only by revitalizing the economy but by bringing people together.

And that's what he wanted.

But right now, he had to deal with his dad.

He zigzagged through the crowd, tugging at the collar of his button-up shirt. When had it gotten so stuffy in here? Even though it was after nine on a Monday night, many people old and young still lingered, and it wouldn't surprise him if they headed to the Frosted Cake for a bite of pie. After congratulating him on a job well done, Madison had ducked out, claiming an early morning at the store.

It was good she was gone, though. Because right now, he needed to get to the truth.

The knot inside Evan was so big it threatened to overwhelm him. Making his way outside, where the cool night air provided some welcome relief, Evan located his dad chatting with a group of men and women near his Lexus in the tiny City Hall parking lot. As he approached, their conversation drifted toward him.

"I hope we can count on all of you to be sponsors for the festival, which I know is going to be a huge success."

"Seems like a great opportunity to come together as a community, Mayor."

Even in the dim light of the City Hall parking lot, Evan could see his dad's eyes twinkle. "That's what we were hoping would happen when we dreamed up this whole thing."

We. Unbelievable. His father was only supporting it now because the whole town seemed behind it. At least he was indeed supporting it.

But there was still something fishy going on. First, Roxy's visit to the store on Saturday. Then, Dad's comment during the council meeting about the *"potential new store going in there."*

Evan kicked a rock across the lot as he marched closer to the group.

His dad angled his head up at Evan's approach. "Ah, and here's my fellow dreamer now. Son, these folks are anxious to support our festival. What do you say to that?"

With a discipline borne of practice, Evan hooked a wide grin that he didn't feel. "That's fantastic, ladies and gentlemen. I don't quite have all the details yet about what sponsorships will entail, but I'm meeting with Ashley Baker this week to start coordinating our efforts and get a committee formed. They will be contacting you within the month to get your support finalized."

The businesspeople smiled and chatted a bit more among themselves, and Evan crept closer to Dad. "We need to talk." The words tasted chalky in his mouth. As much as Evan wanted to get along with his dad, it was quite possible he'd gone too far this time. Evan just had to know for himself.

Slipping on a half-smile, Dad made a show of checking his watch. "I'm sorry, folks, but I promised my wife I'd be home by now. Thank you again for your support."

The crowd said their farewells and disbanded, leaving Evan and his dad alone by the Lexus.

Evan shoved his hands into the pockets of his trousers, and he couldn't help the slump in his shoulders. "Where's Mom?" She almost always attended every public event with Dad.

"She had a headache and stayed home."

"Tell her I hope she feels better soon."

"Will do." Pulling his keys from inside his jacket, his dad spun the key ring around a few times before palming it. "Did you need something else, son?"

Here went nothing. "What new store were you talking about tonight? The one that will bring jobs here?"

His dad studied him for a moment, lips pursed, jaw tight.

Then he nodded to the passenger side of his car. "Get in. I'll give you a ride home."

"I don't live that far." And really, the walk down Main Street and up Park Road in the brisk air sounded just about perfect right now. If he'd had on tennis shoes, Evan might have even jogged it. Anything to get rid of all this pent-up frustration roiling through his body.

"If you want to talk, get in."

As Dad ducked inside his vehicle, Evan resisted the urge to slam his fist against the roof. Instead, he moved to the passenger's side, opened the door, and slid in. "Tell me."

"Watch your tone. I'm still your father." A picture of calm despite the venom seething in his words, his dad adjusted the controls on the dashboard. Heat poured through the vents. Then he put the car into drive and started out of the parking lot.

Evan began to sweat. His fingers itched to roll down his window. "Well? Are you going to tell me?"

Dad kept his eyes on the road. "I'm referring to Herman Hardware. Negotiations are underway once more."

"How can they be? That was my project, and I haven't heard a word from them in weeks."

"Yes, it *was* your project."

"Excuse me?"

Trees flanked the car as his father turned off Main Street and drove up the hill toward Ridge Road. Dad sighed, and the exhaled condescension whisked across the car, smacking Evan in the face. "Aldrin called me last week. He said that Mr. Herman was extremely motivated to open the Walker Beach branch. I'm not certain why."

Evan crossed his arms over his chest. "Then what's your play here? Because from where I'm sitting, that's not going to happen. Madison's store was a hit over the weekend, and I know it'll continue to be."

His dad eased the vehicle into the parking lot of Evan's

apartment complex, which sat flush against the hill, a spectacular view of the ocean and the twinkling lights of downtown spreading out below. He put the car into park and turned in his seat so he faced Evan. "Son, let me ask you something."

The logic in his dad's tone grated against Evan's sensibilities. "OK."

"If you weren't attached to this girl—"

"Madison. Her name is Madison."

"If you weren't attached to Ms. Price, then what would you honestly think is best for this town? A hardware store with a small selection, high prices because of its overhead, and an inexperienced owner who can't afford to hire anyone else? Or one that has promised to hire ten new employees, comes with a catalog of inventory that can be ordered at a competitive price, and has experienced owners who understand business and how to make the right recommendations to buyers, thus resulting in a much more effective store that will bring a lot more money to this community?"

Evan just blinked at his dad. "Madison is still learning. And she's done a fabulous job at it with the time and resources she's had."

"I've not said a word against the girl except what was true. I'm sure she's lovely and a hard worker. I'm just not sure her store is what's best for this town." His dad clapped Evan on the shoulder. "Deep down, you know I'm right. That girl isn't meant to own a hardware store."

She should be a librarian. Evan tried to bat the thought away, but it just sat there, festering against his desire to see Madison succeed.

And Madison wanted to own the hardware store, whether she'd been meant to or not—and what she wanted mattered.

He shook off his dad's hand. "I have to support her." Even if the truth of his dad's words bore into him.

"No, you have to do your job. And your job is doing what's

best for the town. What's going to do more to revitalize Walker Beach? Consider that."

"Dad—"

"Honestly, Evan, if you have any hope of securing that promotion you're itching for, you can't let a trifling thing like lust get in the way of your future." At Evan's attempted protest, he surged on. "No, listen now. I'm sure you're having fun dallying with Ms. Price, but don't allow yourself to get distracted from the real prize, son."

"I'm not *dallying* with her. And Madison *is* the real prize." Evan tamped down the anger simmering in his gut. "I don't have to listen to this." He started to open his door.

"And one more thing."

His hand rested on the door handle. "What?"

"Herman is willing to be a sponsor of the Christmas festival, and the amount he's offering to donate is substantial."

That didn't even make sense. "Why does the guy care so much about this store? Aldrin told us they had several locations they were considering. And why do *you* care so much? The festival is going to be your big win. Did you hear people tonight? They're raving about it, and since you played it off as your idea, you'll get the credit." He tried to keep the resentment from his voice. Tried—and failed.

"But it's not actually happening until after the election, so you can see why I'd like some earlier wins, don't you, son?" Steel sharpened his dad's tone. "Evidence that we're actually helping the town, not just blowing a bunch of money on an event that may or may not result in a better economy."

OK, the heat in the car was just about stifling now. Evan cracked the window, trying to stuff all the emotions brimming to the surface back inside. "We'll find another store that can come in and be a big win for you. And you have other things that you can focus on. Getting the library reopened, securing grants for the other businesses affected by the earthquake. You're doing a lot."

"You know as well as I do that getting another store in here will take months, maybe a year or more. We got lucky that Ms. Chamberlain had connections and made this one happen as quickly as she did. And while the library efforts and other things are all well and good, nothing speaks like money and jobs." His dad's eyes narrowed in on him. "And Herman will provide both of those."

"I think you're exaggerating the boon to our economy that this will have." Evan ran a hand through his hair, gripping the ends before letting go.

"The numbers are there, and they don't lie. Get your head out of the clouds and look over the report again. Compare the benefits of opening Herman Hardware to the benefits your girlfriend's store will provide the town."

He'd had about enough of his dad's patronizing, despite the truth in some of his statements. Evan threw open the door, and a rush of air abated some of the tension in the car. "I don't have the energy for this right now."

"You'd better have energy enough to do your job."

"Dad, what do you want from me? Even if I thought Herman was better for the economy, what am I supposed to do about it? I can't force Madison to close her store." And he wouldn't want her to if it made her happy. Didn't matter if maybe he thought she'd rather be doing something else. That's not what *she* wanted.

"I just need you on board when we bring it to the council for a vote. I'll take care of the rest."

Evan should pry. He should ask what his dad planned to do. But Dad would never tell him.

He was done playing his father's games. Without another word, Evan climbed from the car and slammed the door as hard as he could.

CHAPTER 11

Being among books again—even so many ruined ones —felt every kind of right.

Madison sat on her knees, digging into a box filled with stories of all shapes and sizes. She pulled out the hardback on top, a children's novel with a slightly warped cardboard cover—*My Father's Dragon*. How well she remembered that one. Her nanny had first read it to her when she'd been, what? Six? Seven? The story of a boy named Elmer rescuing a baby dragon in a made-up land had given Madison bravery when she'd faced the monsters under her bed and in her closet. And when she'd faced weeks without the comfort of her parents' arms because they'd been off on one business trip or another.

"How's that one?" Across the room, Ashley sat cross-legged, removing books from her box and sorting them into a keep pile and a toss pile. Her friend stifled a yawn against her hand.

Madison checked the clock on the wall, shocked to see 10:05 staring back at her. They'd been in the basement of Ashley's childhood home for nearly three hours sorting through the library's damaged books. And that after a full day of working in the hardware store. Madison should be passed out on the floor, but instead, extra energy had sizzled to life when she'd entered the place where the library board had stored what was left of the inventory.

"The cover's a bit damaged, but the pages all seem intact." Madison set the book in her keep pile, which held most of the books she'd sorted. The thought of not saving all of them did something to her insides, so she'd rationalized a reason for most of them to end up there. "I don't want to be rude, but . . ."

"Why hasn't this been done before now?"

"Well, yeah. I guess."

"I think I mentioned to you that most of the people on the board are in their seventies or older. They're OK with the mental work—the planning, the petitioning, the brainstorming—but the physical stuff has fallen mostly to me." Ashley blew a stray hair out of her eyes. "I had my family help me haul all of the stuff that was salvageable out of the library after the earthquake, but just haven't had time to do more than that. I appreciate your help so much, Madison. You don't even know."

"Absolutely. Sorry it took me a while to get over here." Now that she *was* here, she couldn't imagine leaving the job to someone else anyway. "I can come back every night this week if you'd like."

"That would be great. I may not be free until nine or so, but I'm sure my parents would be fine with you coming and going as you need to."

Madison cringed as Ashley chucked a book into the toss pile. From here, it looked perfectly acceptable. Maybe she'd sneak over in a bit and rescue it if possible. "So what's the plan when this is done?"

"Once we get an accurate picture of the inventory that's left, we can use the insurance money to purchase more. That's another way your help will be super valuable—you'll have an idea about what books we may need and what people will want to read."

"Don't you think whoever you hire as head librarian may want to do that?"

Evan's whispered words came back to her: *"That sounds right up your alley."* And, yeah, it really did. But she'd committed to a different path, one that included a sure income, not dependence on grant money.

One that honored Chrissy in death, even if Madison hadn't in life.

Ashley fixed her with a strange look. "Maybe, though I don't even know if we'll get the funding for that. Besides, the committee and I are really pushing to get the library reopened within the next month or so. A town shouldn't be without a library for this long." She sighed and leaned back against the brown leather couch behind her. "Of course, we need the perfect space for that to happen. A lot of things have to fall into place. And lately, I haven't had the time to give it the attention it deserves."

Wedding and event season must be picking up. "Well, like I said. Now that the store is running, I'm happy to help. That library meant a lot to me, and I want to see it reopened."

What if . . . But no. Even if the librarian job miraculously became available, she couldn't take it, not after she'd worked so hard to reopen Hole-in-the-Wall. Especially not after Evan had missed out on his opportunity with Herman Hardware because of her.

"We should get you officially on the library board. I'm sure Bud would nominate you." Ashley pulled her legs against her chest and fiddled with a strand of her hair. "So how is it going at the store?"

Madison ran her fingers along the spine of a weathered copy of *Wuthering Heights*. "It's good. I'm still learning." Today she'd made a gaffe when she'd estimated the amount of materials Elizabeth Harding, the owner of Hardings Market, needed for a flooring update. Madison was thankful that the older woman had her double check her pricing, or she'd have charged Elizabeth double what she owed for her order. The situation had sent Madison diving into her copy of *Emma* during her lunch break —an all-too-brief escape.

"So, you like it?"

"As much as I'd like any job." Well, maybe not *any* job. "But I'm sure Chrissy had her days too. Being a business owner is stressful and a lot of responsibility. I'll settle into it. You'll see when you start your wedding planning business."

"If I ever start it."

"You will. And you'll do great."

"Thanks, but I can hardly keep my head above water now with everything my boss has me doing plus the library stuff. And now Evan is tapping me to help with the Christmas Festival, which I'm more than happy to do. With all that, the business is probably going to be sidelined for a bit." Ashley resumed sorting the books from her box. "Back to you. I'm glad you feel like running the store is going well. But . . ."

It wasn't like her friend to be so hesitant. Or somber. "But what? Just say it, Ash."

"I sometimes wonder if you're sad you gave up your dream of being a librarian."

The books in Madison's keep pile threatened to topple. Was she so obvious? She removed the top three and set them neatly next to the others. "Sometimes, I guess. But I've worked so hard to get the store going, and I do think Chrissy would be proud of all I've accomplished. You know, facing my fears, staying here . . ."

"Dating Evan Walsh." But instead of the grin Madison would have expected to slick across Ashley's face at the statement, she couldn't miss the way her friend bit her bottom lip.

"That too."

"Madison, are you sure about him? About all of it?"

"Where is this coming from?" Madison tugged at the sleeves

of her sweatshirt. "I thought you said he'd changed. That he was a good guy."

"I think he is, but I just want to be sure *you* think so. The last time we talked, you didn't seem so certain."

Funny to think there was ever a time when she hadn't been completely sure of him. "I do think so. In fact, I know so."

"And all of this—the store, Evan, staying in Walker Beach—it's what you really want? Because I know a little something about regret, and believe me, you don't want to live with it."

Madison studied her friend who always seemed so positive. What did Ashley have to regret? But the way Ashley's hands curled into fists told Madison that maybe now wasn't the time to ask.

However, she *could* answer Ashley's question. "The only thing I know for sure is that I would regret not staying and trying. I have regrets too—mostly, that I didn't come home, that I wasn't here when Aunt Chrissy needed me. And you're right. Regret is a terrible thing to live with."

"I guess all we can do is live with our decisions and learn from them, right?"

"Yeah, I guess so." Madison stroked the once-intact cover of the book in her hands, now crisp and brittle from the floodwaters. She frowned. Not even her desire to save all the books could rescue this one from the toss pile.

CHAPTER 12

If she hurried, she'd be able to catch Evan before he left the office.

Madison flipped the sign on Hole-in-the-Wall's door to Closed, locked up, and doused the lights in the front of the store then strode to the kitchen to grab the cookies she'd made and bagged last night. Her eyes caught the time on the microwave—7:01 p.m.—and she picked up the pace. Evan had mentioned he'd be staying late at work most nights this week, and Tuesday would be no exception.

As she left the store, Madison skipped down the boardwalk. A smattering of late-winter tourists dotted the beach, most donning sweaters and jeans rolled to mid-calf as they walked barefoot in the sand. Still, there were fewer than usual this time of year, when all the cold-state residents sought out the warmth of the California beaches. But if Evan's festival were a success like he thought it'd be, she hoped by this time next year things would be back to normal.

Pride swelled in her chest as she made her way toward City Hall. She hadn't seen much of him since the town council meeting just over a week ago, but that was only natural when he was in the throes of planning. Even though she'd filled her evenings with book sorting and a few other library-related tasks Ashley had for her, Madison was surprised how much she missed him. All day she'd been anticipating this moment, when she could come by and show her support with cookies and a few kisses.

Madison's phone trilled from her back pocket, breaking the peace of the setting. Gripping the bag of cookies in one hand, she grabbed for the phone with the other and saw a number she didn't recognize. Before owning the store, she'd have ignored it, but it might be one of her suppliers or someone asking for information about the store's offerings—though she had to admit, it was an unusual time to be calling. "Hello?"

"Hi, is this Madison Price?" The woman on the other end spoke in a brisk, business-like tone.

"Yes. And who is this?"

"My name is Carol Davenport. You inherited Chrissy Price's store on Main Street in Walker Beach, correct?"

Madison scoured her memory for the woman's name but couldn't place it. "Yes."

"I'm your landlord, then." No warmth emanated from Carol's tone, only frigid professionalism.

"Oh. Wonderful. I've been meaning to call you and update you on the situation." Just one of the many things that had fallen by the wayside when she'd decided to reopen Hole-in-the-Wall. She did know she had at least a few months left on the lease, so she hadn't worried about the details just yet.

"Do you have a moment right now?" A clattering of computer keyboard keys filled the space between them. "There's something we need to discuss."

This sounded like it might take a while, and she was only about a minute from City Hall. Madison veered off the boardwalk toward the ocean and plopped onto the sand. The full moon was huge tonight, pushing the stars out of the way like a diva on stage. "Sure. What's up?" Madison cleared her throat. "I mean, how can I help you?"

"Your lease is up in sixty-three days, and I regret to inform you that I will not be renewing the agreement that I formed with your aunt."

Waves crashed onto the sand just beyond Madison. "What do you mean?"

"Just what I said. I am required by law to give you sixty days' notice if I am not renewing the lease, and I am choosing not to renew it."

Goosebumps popped all over Madison's arms, as if the ocean had doused her. "But my family has been renting that space for fifty-some years."

A pause. "Yes, well, I've decided to end that agreement. And while it's unfortunate for you, it's fully within my right to do so."

"Do you want more money for it or something? I can . . ." But she had no right to promise that she'd be able to pay more. While numbers from her first full week of sales had been strong —the townspeople had really shown up in support of her— there was no guarantee they'd remain that way.

"Unfortunately, no amount you can offer me will be sufficient."

"I . . . I don't understand." Madison's brain hurt. It was all she could do to reign in her emotions and not yell at the woman for the unfairness of it all. "Why are you doing this?"

Carol sighed. "It's not personal. It's business. And right now, I have to think about what's best for mine." A muffled voice filled the background. "I'm sorry, Ms. Price, I need to go. And I am sorry for having to deliver this bad news to you. I'll overnight the necessary documents tomorrow so you'll have everything in writing."

The line died, and Madison stared at the phone. What was she going to do now?

The cellophane bag of cookies rustled in her lap. Evan.

Madison stood. Yes, Evan would know how to help. Maybe she could lease one of the open spaces next to her store for even cheaper than her current rent. The mayor had indicated that those spaces might not be available, but maybe they were now. Thinking about how much work the move would be nearly halted her in her tracks, but she put one foot in front of the other and held her tears of frustration at bay until she reached Evan's office and knocked.

"Come in."

She shoved open the door, and the sight of him hunched behind his desk, a half-eaten salad beside him, slammed her with affection. No, more than affection.

Love.

Whoa. How had she gone from no connection to anyone, standing on her own, to running to someone when she was hurting—to *loving* someone—all in a matter of weeks?

Life was strange. And also, despite the heartaches, beautiful.

"Madison? What's wrong?"

Shaking herself free from her thoughts—and remembering why she'd come in the first place—Madison closed the door behind her and walked toward him. He met her halfway, pulling her into a secure hug, squishing the bag of cookies between them.

"I need your help." The words got lost as she mumbled them into his white button-up shirt.

He grasped her upper arms gently and waited for her to look up at him. "What happened?"

Madison's breath shuddered in and out while she relayed her landlord's phone call. As the story unfolded, Evan's face grew paler and paler. "What did you say her name was again?"

"Carol Davenport."

"Davenport." Evan strode back to his desk, slid into his chair, and focused on his computer screen while he clicked and typed.

Madison joined him, dropping the cookies onto his abnormally messy desk and settling her hands on his firm shoulders.

After a few moments, he sat back and sighed. "Looks like she is from Walker Beach originally but now lives in Los Angeles and inherited the property from a relative." Evan grabbed Madison's hand and rotated his chair, pulling her onto his lap.

"I just don't get why she'd do this." She looped her arms around his neck and brought her head to rest on his shoulder.

His lightly stubbled chin brushed her forehead as he tucked his hands around her waist. "I think it's my dad's doing."

Her head popped up. "What do you mean?"

Evan's brow furrowed. "Last week, he all but told me he had a plan to oust you from your store. I've scoured my brain trying to figure it out, but I never thought he'd go after your lease agreement."

"Why would he do that?"

"Plenty of reasons, all of them coming down to greed and pride. I wouldn't put it past him to have made an agreement with Herman that would grease his palms or get some campaign donations. Something. With him, it could be anything. And maybe he just wants to stick it to me, as well." Now Evan just looked plain miserable.

"Surely your dad wouldn't do that."

"You don't know him like I do."

Despite how much she was hurting, she hated that Evan was taking some of this on himself. Madison absently ran her thumb along the edge of Evan's ear, following his strong jawline down toward his chin. She leaned in and gave him a quick peck on the lips. "This isn't your fault. And I'm not giving up. Maybe I need to just make a trek to Los Angeles and chat with Ms. Davenport in person. We should be able to work something out."

The plan sounded weak even to her, so she wasn't surprised when Evan fixed her with a disbelieving stare. "I'm willing to bet that my dad and Herman are either renting the space from her or paying her a lot of money not to rent it to you."

"Can they do that?"

"Maybe not officially, and they wouldn't be dumb enough to leave a trail." He squeezed her waist. "I'll do what I can to find out this week, OK?"

"I appreciate that more than you know, but I don't want to distract you with my problems. You're busy with the festival." Madison waved her hand toward Evan's desk, which was piled high with papers. She started to turn her head, but before she could, her eyes registered the words across the topmost page.

She shifted in Evan's lap, reaching for the paper and pulling it close to examine it.

"Oh, that's confiden—"

"Herman Hardware Versus Hole-in-the-Wall Hardware: An Economic Comparison?" Madison turned to face Evan again. "What's this?"

Evan's jaw tensed, and he snatched the multipage report from her. "It's nothing, Madison. Believe me."

"Did you create that report? Please tell me it's weeks old." But the fact it had been at the top of the pile . . .

Was he behind the call from the landlord?

No. He wouldn't do that. So why this sense of betrayal crawling up her throat?

He scrubbed a hand down his face. "Please, Madison, it's—"

"Just tell me the truth." She kept accusation out of her voice. Still, she hopped off his lap to clear her head of the fog created by their physical chemistry. "I'm sure you have a good explanation."

Evan leaned forward in his chair, elbows on his knees and hands covering his mouth. Finally, after what seemed like hours, he straightened and looked Madison in the eye. "My dad asked me to really think about which store was better for our economy. Because on the surface, it seems like yours. But when I really dove into the numbers"—he looked away—"I didn't want it to be true, but it does seem like Herman Hardware would be better long-term for Walker Beach."

"Why are you doing that analysis now? I thought this was over."

"It was. It should have been. But Dad is persistent. And he reminded me that doing what's best for the town is part of my job—and part of the head community developer's job. Please understand, Madison, it's not personal." He reached for her hand.

She wrenched away before he could touch her. "People keep saying that. But this is my family's business. What's more personal than that?"

"You're right. I'm sorry. But Mad"—Evan stood and turned her around to face him—"do you hear yourself? You called it your family's business. Not yours."

"So?"

"So . . . I don't know. You're doing great with it, but are you happy?"

"And what do you know about being happy, Evan?" Hurt twisted on his face, but she turned off her fount of sympathy. "You gave up baseball, the one thing you love—whether to please or spite your father, I'm not certain. But are you really happy in this job? Is this what you always dreamed of? Dressing up day in and day out, staying behind a computer, schmoozing and being in the middle of town politics?"

"It's not that bad. It's a solid job. And I'm good at it." He was quiet for a moment. "Baseball isn't an option for me, not anymore. But we're not talking about me. We're talking about you. Wouldn't you rather do the thing you went to school for? I've been chatting with Ashley, and we think we could get you the head librarian job if you wanted it."

"Oh, so you're talking about me behind my back now?" A momentary jolt of intrigue, of pleasure, hit her at the thought of taking over the librarian duties for the town. But no. For several reasons, she'd already resolved to stick it out with the store. She couldn't give up now—especially not for some job that might never materialize. "I'm going to find a way to keep the store open. I came here for your help. Are you going to help me or not?"

Indecision warred on his face, but his hesitation said it all. "I want to . . ."

Once again, the person she'd trusted, the guy she'd allowed to glimpse the real her—the one she'd allowed herself to fall in love with, for goodness' sake—wasn't standing up for her.

Which meant that, once again, Madison was on her own.

"Goodbye, Evan." She turned on her heel and managed to march from the room, down the front steps of City Hall, and across the street to the beach before she burst into tears. Having no one to hold her up, she crumpled, sinking down into the sand.

She'd known—known!—people couldn't be trusted to fight her battles for her. Yet she'd stupidly allowed herself to open her heart to Evan. To the whole town, really.

If only she'd left. Or, at the very least, had kept to herself. Maybe the store would have opened a bit later, but her heart wouldn't feel like someone had ripped it from her chest and tossed it into the waves to be pummeled by the sea.

Madison slapped at her tears, closing her eyes against them until her tear ducts burned with the effort. When she'd schooled her emotions into submission, she stood on wobbly legs—but stood, on her own, all the same—and stumbled home.

CHAPTER 13

It didn't matter how hard he had fought.

Evan Walsh had lost.

"Why do you look so sad? This is a major accomplishment for you."

Roxy's whisper penetrated Evan's thoughts as they watched Hank Aldrin flourish his signature across the official agreement that would bring Herman Hardware to Walker Beach. Sitting next to Hank, Evan's dad took the pen and added his John Hancock. Just beyond the men's place behind the table in the council chambers of City Hall, a few members of the local press and town residents gathered for the signing and press conference.

As members of the team who had helped the agreement come to fruition, Evan and Roxy stood behind and to the side of the front table along with the other members of the town council. Just being here felt like a betrayal to Madison, but what could Evan do? As his dad had reminded him, this was his job—to see that Walker Beach thrived as much as possible.

He'd never hated his job more.

"Seriously, Evan. Without you, this wouldn't be happening."

At his ex-girlfriend's hiss, Evan shot her a quick glare. "Don't remind me." Yeah, most people would be proud, but most people hadn't ruined the one true thing they'd finally had in their life.

He was pathetic.

As his father clapped Hank Aldrin on the shoulder, touting all the benefits this union would bring, the self-loathing in Evan's mind deepened. When Madison had come to him last week, he should have done things differently. Should have marched right over to Dad's house and told him he'd known what he did.

But the tiny bit of doubt had niggled him. What if he were wrong? What if the landlord situation wasn't actually a setup but a happy blessing that allowed him to proceed with the Herman Hardware agreement and show Madison that she was better off doing something else with her time?

And what if his false accusations tore down the already weak bridge that he and his dad had finally built?

Furthermore, Herman Hardware *was* actually best for the town. The report hadn't lied. He'd gone over it again and again. Of course, if the company were so corrupt it would stoop to surreptitiously taking out the competition, that wasn't one he wanted in Walker Beach. Reports didn't take everything into account.

Whatever the case, Evan didn't have the answers. So all week long, he'd kept quiet, stuck his head in the sand, and worked on other projects. Figured that maybe if he stayed out of it, he could keep a clear conscience. But then, on Monday, the council had added a last-minute addition to the agenda—approval of the agreement between Herman and Walker Beach. Bud had voted against the measure, but the rest of the council, including Dad, had approved it without hesitation.

As the press conference concluded and Hank Aldrin walked over to shake Evan's hand, he knew that being an ostrich was just as much a betrayal to Madison as signing the agreement himself.

"Thanks for all the work you did on this, Evan. Roxy was right about you." As Aldrin placed his beefy hand in Evan's, he winked at a blushing Roxy—boy, she could turn it on when she wanted to. She bowed out of the conversation and turned to chat with a reporter. "If you ever get tired of Walker Beach and want to join us in the city, you give me a shout. You're just the kind of man I like working with."

"Thank you, sir." Once, he might have been flattered. But what did Aldrin see in him, really? Was it that he'd worked harder than a dog on his presentations and analyses? Or that he'd been willing to throw over the woman he loved for—

Wait. Loved?

No. He didn't . . .

But she was the one person who hadn't asked him to be someone he wasn't. Who challenged him to be better than this laced-up, perfect specimen of business acumen that he was trying to be. Who brought joy to his life just by being in it.

And if that wasn't love, what was?

Oh man. He'd messed up even worse than he'd realized.

His dad strutted over in his three-piece suit, nudging Aldrin with an elbow. "Are you over here trying to steal my head community developer away?"

Evan straightened. "What?"

"That's right. The entire council agrees you're the man for the job."

"I don't know what to say." Evan kept his voice steady, but on the inside, he longed to leap in the air, fist pump, shout.

And call Madison.

The good news of his promotion soured in his gut.

Aldrin slapped him on the back. "Well, congratulations, Walsh. Guess I'm too late. Thought you may enjoy a bit of the corporate life, that's all. Most young men do. Old men too." His eyebrows waggled in Roxy's direction, and Evan guessed the implications. "Let me know if you ever change your mind."

The man turned and joined Roxy in chatting with the reporter. Evan couldn't help but notice how close Aldrin stood to her, his hand skimming her lower back. How she glanced up at her boss, flicking a grin his way despite the hollowness in her eyes.

Evan turned away, a sick feeling roiling through his stomach. Maybe her behavior should disgust him, but was he really any better, doing what he had to do—making deals with devils—to get what he wanted? Or what he'd thought he'd wanted, anyway.

Dad sidled up to Evan and cleared his throat. "I know I don't say it often, son, but I'm proud of the hard work you put in to make this happen."

Evan's jaw fell.

The mayor clasped Evan's upper arm and continued. "You've proven yourself to me, Evan. And I won't forget it. In fact, I mean to see you win Bud's seat in the upcoming election. As you know, he's not running again. And I want you beside me. You have a great future in politics and in this town."

He had absolutely no interest in politics, and it seemed like a conflict of interest for the head community developer to also own a seat on the city council, but he couldn't tear his eyes away from the pride shining in Dad's. Finally, his father saw before him a man he could respect. Evan hated how all of this had wounded Madison—and would probably never forgive himself for his role in that hurt—but maybe there was still a chance his relationship with his dad could be redeemed despite it all.

"Thanks for your confidence in me. I'll have to think about it." Just the fact his dad wanted Evan beside him, though. Man.

Dad led him toward an empty corner of the room. "And now that you've earned my full trust, there's a matter we need to discuss. I can give you more details in the office tomorrow, but, essentially, we need to delay the library reopening for six months."

"Why would we do that?" At the next town council meeting, Ashley was planning to present the finalized budget for the library reopening, and Evan was submitting his recommendation for the next-quarter grant funding.

"Between you and me, I may have promised a grant to Joe Meyer."

"The owner of the golf course?"

His dad nodded. "And we have some wiggle room in the budget if we delay the library opening a bit."

Evan stared at his dad. "The golf course is doing fine. It doesn't need a grant. That money is for struggling businesses and government entities, like the library, that need help after the earthquake."

"Joe wants to do some remodeling."

"Remodeling. Right." A caustic laugh slipped out. "Why would you promise a grant to someone? That's my department. My job."

Dad waved his hand in the air. "And you're my son. I knew you'd support me. And Joe's support, in turn, will help me win the election."

Unbelievable. "So all this talk about getting Bud's spot on the council is not because you actually believe in me but because I'll give you my loyalty."

"Lower your voice, son. And yes, you've proven your loyalty to me. Why wouldn't you want that rewarded?"

Didn't his dad understand? Evan didn't care two licks about the power. He'd wanted people's respect, not this. "I—"

"I knew you'd understand. I've got to run, but I fully expect you to take care of this. All right, son? Good." And with that, his dad was off, melding into the crowd so he could schmooze with the townspeople.

Evan's head ached, but his stomach hurt worse. He needed a

quick getaway in case he hurled. If only that would purge his system from the filth that covered his soul. Sure, this was small potatoes compared to what other politicians dabbled in, but still . . .

Shoving his hands into his pockets, Evan pulled out his keys and strode toward the parking lot.

"Evan!"

He turned.

Alex jogged toward him. "You all right, man? You looked kind of sick in there."

"Just a lot on my mind." His head continued to spin. "I've gotta go. See you at the office tomorrow."

"All right." Alex's eyebrows pushed together as he studied Evan. "Drive safe, OK? And let me know if there's anything I can do to help."

"Thanks, buddy. I will." Evan climbed into his truck and drove out of town, hopping on the highway going north and continuing around the bends and curves that hugged the ocean for what seemed like hours. His heart felt ready to leap from his chest, pounding with emotions he couldn't name.

How had he found himself here? His intentions had been good. With Chrissy's encouragement, he'd turned his life around.

So how had he still ended up as someone who hurt others for his own gain? Maybe he'd always be the forever-broken screw-up desperate for approval.

"Argh!" He smacked the dashboard. The pulse of resulting pain radiated through his palm and up his arm. Evan pulled onto a shoulder of the road and leaned his head against his window. His vehicle was perched on a precipice looking out over the sea. Above him, the moon peeked from behind a handful of clouds, shining its light here and there, unpredictable.

Where was Evan going? He was on the road, aimless. Lost.

But Madison, she'd been the one to help him find his way, to remind him that he didn't have to be anyone but Evan Walsh to garner her affection. He had to get back to her. Had to do whatever it took to show her how much he cared about her, how much he needed her.

How much he'd always needed her, even back in high school when he'd written her those stupid letters.

He whipped his truck around and drove as quickly as he dared, not stopping until he got to her house. After knocking for what seemed like ages, he headed for the store. Again, no one answered his persistent knocks. Evan lifted his phone to his ear and called her phone, but it went straight to voicemail.

Maybe Ashley knew where she was. He dialed, jumping into the conversation before Ashley could finish her greeting. "Hey, is Madison with you?"

A pause. "Evan?"

"Yeah. Is Madison there? I really need to talk to her."

"No." Another hesitation. "She's gone, Evan. She went back to Los Angeles."

No way. She wouldn't have just left. Her store was still here. Her house. *He* was still here.

But clearly, she'd written him out of her life. Just like in high school, she'd assumed the worst about him and left. Only this time, she'd been right.

It was time to accept the truth. Maybe the worst *was* the truth.

If a good woman like Madison didn't believe Evan Walsh was worth sticking around for, then—despite all his good intentions—maybe he really wasn't.

CHAPTER 14

"Thanks for coming in today, Madison." The woman pushed her tortoise-shell glasses up the bridge of her nose. "It was a pleasure to meet you. If I have my way, you'll be getting a job offer by the end of business tomorrow."

The news should have made her happy, so Madison forced a cheerful tone. "Thank you so much." Madison held out her hand, and Darshell shook it. "I look forward to hearing from you."

They stood and exited Darshell's small office, emerging into the main part of the massive bookstore close to downtown Los Angeles. Floor-to-ceiling shelves with the hottest new books surrounded her, and the bright lighting accentuated their colorful covers. Her pre-interview sweep of the place had revealed plush leather brown and red chairs tucked away in all the cozy corners, encouraging shoppers to escape into a world of wonder right here. It was most definitely Madison's kind of place.

But while the smells—fresh paper and ink, mingled with the hint of coffee in the air—were familiar, this place still didn't strike a chord of longing in her.

Not like the current pangs directing her back to Walker Beach.

But that wasn't an option, not if she didn't have the hardware store. Yeah, she could fight for it. But a sense of barrenness had settled in her heart from all the striving, all the wishing. All the disappointment. So she'd put a Closed sign on the door and hightailed it out of town the morning after she'd heard from the landlord.

The morning after Evan had broken her heart. Again.

"Feel free to hang out here, get a feel for the store," Darshell said. "Tony at the coffee shop can give you a free latte on the house, if that's your thing. Or tea. Or a muffin. Whatever. Just let him know to use the comp code."

"That's so generous." Madison's stomach rumbled at the suggestion, and her hands flew to her midsection, a blush attacking her cheeks.

Darshell smiled and headed back into her office.

For several minutes, Madison wandered the store. The display up front reminded her that Valentine's Day was on Monday. Inwardly, she groaned. She and Evan had made plans to celebrate together after his council meeting. He'd promised to take care of everything.

And now, she'd be here, in Los Angeles, alone in the tiny apartment of an acquaintance who was currently out of town and had agreed to sublet to Madison if she would be staying.

Alone was her *modus operandi*. It had served her well for many years, and she just needed to remember that when her heart yearned for Walker Beach.

For Evan.

"Stop it."

At her whispered self-rebuke, an employee with a man bun glanced up from his re-shelving work and lifted a pierced eyebrow in her direction.

Clearing her throat, Madison hurried to the next shelving

unit around the corner, pretending to peruse the book spines. If she were going to work here, talking to herself wasn't the best first impression. Yeah, working in a bookstore making minimum wage wasn't her dream job, but she hoped it would only be temporary.

Emily, an acquaintance from grad school, had made inquiries for Madison with some librarians she knew about potential jobs but nothing sounded overly promising. Madison had already been online and applied for the paltry number of jobs she could find. If she could only snag one that was funded with grant money, so be it. Beggars couldn't be choosers. Maybe she just needed to accept that sure things didn't exist.

Maybe that's why Evan's betrayal had stung so much—she'd finally started believing that she could count on him, that he'd never let her down.

For the second time, her stomach protested her lack of food today, so Madison headed to the coffee shop and ordered a passion iced tea and a premade chicken salad sandwich. Skipping the use of Darshell's promo code, Madison paid and whisked out the door and into the fading sunshine of a Californian day. The bookstore was only a short distance from the beach, so she followed the winding sidewalk toward the sand and found a spot that wasn't overly crowded.

Close by, a group of people readied a pile of wood, stacking it into the telltale tented structure necessary for a beach bonfire. Several of them laughed and chatted, their scattered words floating toward her on the breeze. While some worked on lighting the fire, others pulled sticks, hot dogs, and marshmallows from their coolers and bags.

Unwrapping her sandwich and taking a bite, Madison watched the sun sink against the horizon. The bread was soggy, melding in her mouth with the wet chicken, but Madison was too hungry to protest. When she was done, she pulled her knees against her chest and rested her chin on top to ward off the sudden chill of the early evening.

The last time she'd been on the beach at night, Evan had been with her.

She tried to push the errant thought from her mind, but Madison found herself thinking about the way he'd wrapped his arm around her waist, tugging her close against him, sharing his warmth after a long day of exhausting work.

What was he doing right now? Was he just as miserable as she was, or was he spending his Friday night in a much better way? Maybe he'd already moved on from her, finding comfort in female companionship with a homegrown Walker Beach girl, someone who truly belonged there—not someone who only wished she did.

OK, time to get off this beach and bury herself in a good book. That always took the edge off. But Madison found her eyes mesmerized by the undulating flames of the now-lit bonfire. She couldn't look away from the friends who had gathered there. One woman strummed a guitar and sang, her hypnotic voice numbing Madison's will to move.

And then, in the stillness, a memory surfaced. Was it freshman year? Sophomore? Aunt Chrissy had found out that students from the high school were getting together for a bonfire after a football game one Friday night, and she'd asked whether Madison would be joining them.

"Um, no. I'm not even going to the game." Madison planned to stay home and snuggle up with the latest John Green novel. She even had a box of tissues nearby, anticipating the book's sure ability to tug at her heartstrings.

"Hmm." It was all her aunt said, but Madison knew it signaled her disapproval. Still, Aunt Chrissy didn't say anything else about it.

That evening, her aunt interrupted her reading and asked if Madison would like to join her for a walk. Madison wanted to say no, but she couldn't refuse the look on her aunt's hopeful face. After all,

Aunt Chrissy hadn't asked to be burdened with a social outcast for a niece. And some fresh air might not be the worst thing in the world.

But as they walked, veering toward the beach, Madison grew suspicious. As a roaring fire came into view, she nearly put on the brakes. Before she could, though, Aunt Chrissy turned to her. "Let's sit for a minute, shall we?"

It's not like they were close to the fire, but even just being out here—seeing her fellow students teasing, pushing, shrieking playfully, singing, eating—it all twisted her insides into a knot of . . . what? Surely not longing. She'd had the chance to go and hadn't. Of course, it's not like she'd had anyone to go with. Her only real friend, Ashley, was too caught up with her fellow cross-country teammates these days to spend any time with Madison.

Glad her aunt couldn't hear her thoughts, Madison begrudgingly sat next to her in the soft sand. For several minutes, they didn't speak, just listened to the ocean lapping, the tug of the waves going in, going out. But even the ocean couldn't drown out the laughter of the students down the beach.

"Madison." Aunt Chrissy turned toward her niece. The moonlight softened the sharp point of her nose, illuminating the fine lines around her mouth and the corners of her eyes—smile lines, because her aunt was so often happy. "Are you cold?"

OK, that's not what she'd expected her to say.

Was she cold? "I guess." The temperature must have lowered slowly because until this moment, she hadn't noticed.

Her aunt hesitated then looped an arm through Madison's.

At first, Madison stiffened. Her aunt knew she wasn't a fan of physical contact. But after a minute or two, she began to melt against Chrissy. There was something so real, so comforting in her touch.

"You know, as a kid, fire scared me."

Huh? What was Aunt Chrissy talking about?

"Whenever my family went camping, I'd sit as far away as I possibly could, terrified I'd get burned."

Madison glanced at Aunt Chrissy, whose eyes were transfixed on the bonfire. Oh. She was about to get all metaphorical on Madison. "Aunt Chrissy . . ." But she stopped and let her aunt continue. It wasn't like she could have stopped her anyway.

Aunt Chrissy squeezed Madison's arm with a light touch. "My brother—your dad—made fun of me, but I wouldn't budge. Inevitably, though, I'd start to get cold, and I'd complain. And my mom would say, 'If you'd only move closer to the fire, you'd be warm.'"

"But you weren't wrong. Fires can *burn you." The instant the words were out of her mouth, Madison grimaced. She'd played right into Aunt Chrissy's hand with that one.*

"They can. But they usually don't." Her aunt paused, inhaling deeply the brackish scent permeating the air. "People may disappoint you, Madison, and that's a risk we take in relationships. But there is also great joy to be found in closeness with others. If you spend your life afraid of the flames, you'll never know the true warmth of love."

The memory drifted away on the same breeze that carried the woodsy scent of fire to tickle Madison's nose.

Oh, how she missed her aunt. Madison had taken her wisdom, her love, for granted. Chrissy Price had given and given but had never given up—not on Madison and not on anyone else who had hurt or disappointed her. How had she done it?

Love had been a greater motivator than fear, hurt, and anger.

Was it really as simple as that?

And if that were true, was it something that Madison could embrace in her own life? Could she consciously choose to forgive, to believe the best about people—about Evan—and run toward something instead of away from the fear chasing her?

Madison had complained for years about Walker Beach, had blamed the people there for her problems. But what if the real source of her problems was . . . her?

Snippets of moments since she'd returned swept over her—sweet times with Bud and Ms. Josephine and Mrs. Wildman and Ashley and, yes, Evan. These people had simply embraced and accepted Madison for who she was. Not who she'd been, not even who her aunt had been.

Just like Aunt Chrissy had all along, they'd welcomed Madison with open arms into their town, into their lives.

And now she had a choice—to run away, taking a job in Los Angeles that meant nothing to her because it was safe, or to risk the flames for the possibility of warmth.

For the possibility of love.

How had he circled back to this?

Music pulsed life into the building, but Evan was dead inside. The Friday night crush of people—mostly twenty-somethings from Walker Beach with only partying on their minds—had ebbed and flowed in the two hours since Evan had sat here at this bar. Smells of all sorts permeated the air, chicken wings and booze being the strongest. He'd already been approached by at least five women who had flirted and offered to do more than buy him a drink.

The scene at the Canteen was a familiar one, one he'd lived for many years of his life. Back then, he was the life of the party, dancing with a new woman every night as he raised a shot in the air and threw it back, whooping for another.

But being familiar and being comforting were not the same thing.

Still, if this was who Evan truly was, then maybe he just needed to get over himself and accept it.

He stared at the seven-ounce glass in front of him on the counter. The ice had melted, diluting the whiskey on the inside. Evan reached for it for the tenth time in as many minutes, running his fingertips along the streaks of condensation on the outside of the old-fashioned glass. He imagined the slow burn that would trail all the way down to his gut. The self-loathing that would follow.

But could he really loathe himself more than he already did? At least if he drank it away, he'd forget it for a time.

Fingers trembling, he lifted the glass toward his lips.

"I don't think you want to do that, son."

He nearly dropped the glass at the sudden intrusion into his world and turned to find Bud Travis on the stool next to him.

In all his time here, he'd never once seen Mr. Travis, who went to church every Sunday and was so obviously in love with his wife that every year he took out an ad in the paper on Valentine's Day proclaiming it.

"Bud?"

Bud waved down the bartender and ordered a club soda with lime then turned wary eyes on Evan. "I know what you're thinking, and you're right. This isn't exactly my usual hangout."

"So why are you here?"

The bar's owner got on the mic and declared the start of karaoke. The crowd met his announcement with enthusiastic applause.

Bud waited to answer, receiving his drink order in the meantime. He took a sip. "Do you remember my grandson, Colin? He must have been about your year in school."

"Vaguely. He was ahead of me." He'd been one of the smart kids, so he and Evan hadn't shared many of the same classes. "Didn't he go to Harvard or something?"

"Yes, he graduated high school early and flew through his undergraduate program then attended med school at Yale. Brilliant boy." Bud tapped his temple. "Up here, anyway."

What did any of this have to do with the reason Bud was at the Canteen tonight? Evan's brow furrowed, but he stayed quiet.

"You can imagine my surprise when, last year, I heard Colin had been let go from his residency program for being drunk on the job." The lines of Bud's face, the narrowing of his eyes, revealed his pain at the revelation.

"Man, I'm sorry." The words stuck in Evan's throat, but he couldn't let the man's vulnerability go unnoticed. "That's rough."

"Thank you. But I'm not telling you this for sympathy, merely as an explanation." Downing the rest of his beverage, Bud's assessing eyes seemed to take in all of Evan—not just his disheveled hair, unshaven jaw, and rumpled clothing but the state of his soul too. "Ever since the incident with Colin, I come here a few times a month and take a good long look around. Just to see if I notice anyone in need of . . . encouragement."

Encouragement. Ha. Most of the people here would have scoffed at Bud's offer, but something twisted inside Evan's gut.

His eyes perused the bar. Two women headed up to the stage, swaying on their feet in that pretty-buzzed-but-not-yet-wasted way. A poppy tune pumped through the house, and the pair broke into an off-tune rendition of "Oops, I Did It Again." At one time, Evan would have been in the front row, letting his eyes roam the women's overexposed chests and waiting to take one of them home.

All he wanted at this moment, though? To find Madison, to spend time watching old movies with her on the couch, letting her fall asleep in his arms as the credits rolled. But she'd left for good. Her quiet slipping away had spoken loudly about her feelings toward Evan.

And he couldn't blame her one bit.

"So, tonight it's my turn?" Evan stared at the drink, willing himself to pick it up and down it in one fell swoop, to blur the edges of the emotions coursing through him. "Thank you for offering encouragement, but you'd be wasting it on me. See, I've already been encouraged. Chrissy Price took an interest in helping me change. And it worked. For a little while."

How disappointed Chrissy would be if she could see him

now. Maybe she was watching him from heaven, had seen how he'd hurt her niece. Maybe it was better she wasn't here to see how far he'd fallen from the person she'd wanted him to be.

"Change isn't a one-and-done thing, son."

How was the affection so much more apparent in Bud's voice when he called him son compared with Evan's own father?

Bud tugged at the end of his beard as he studied Evan with eyebrows drawn together. "It's something that requires us to constantly be on our guard. Our old nature can easily come creeping back in if we aren't careful. We have to use the resources we've been given to fight against the old us. And aside from faith, one of the greatest resources we have is the people who love us."

"What happens when you betray the people who love you?" Did Madison love him? He'd never know now.

Evan's lips shook as he lifted the glass of whiskey to them. He held it there, not tipping it back, just feeling the cold of the rim against his mouth. He longed to be numbed, not to feel this gnawing ache of failure in his chest anymore.

Yet he knew from experience that this wasn't going to work.

Which somehow left him feeling even more hollow.

Evan slammed the glass back onto the counter, surprised it didn't shatter into a thousand pieces at the force.

Bud placed a wrinkled hand on Evan's forearm. "Real love forgives, son. Seventy times seven."

"And what if I can't forgive myself?" He raked a hand across his face, suddenly afraid that the tears building behind his eyes were going to come spilling out, embarrassing him even more than his little outburst already had.

"I learned a long time ago that often it's ourselves we have the hardest time forgiving. But then I realized something—you have to redefine success and failure."

"What do you mean?" He glanced up at Bud.

"We will always fail in life. That's a given. But it's the getting back up, the trying again, the trying to be better that defines success because it's in those times we build character. You've failed, sure, but that doesn't mean you're destined for *this* life." He gestured around the bar, at the glass of whiskey on the counter. "Don't stop fighting for what you want, and you will have taken one more step toward being the man you want to be."

What did Evan really want? He'd thought it was respect, maybe even love from his father. But being respected by a man like him was actually the opposite of what he should be after.

Instead, he wanted to be able to look himself in the mirror.

And then, an idea bloomed—a way to prove to them all, but most of all to himself, that he was indeed one step closer to being who he longed to be.

Oh man. But what it would take . . .

"The biggest changes take the biggest leaps of faith. And the most courage." Chrissy's voice, her smile as she'd said the words, came back to him. They'd been sitting in her living room, Chrissy on the couch where she'd spent her last days, Evan in the recliner next to it. She'd just informed him that she'd decided to switch from fighting the illness to inviting hospice into her home.

Remembering how fiercely she'd fought, how fiercely she'd loved, he couldn't help the tear that coursed down his cheek. Then he straightened and pushed the glass in front of him far out of reach.

If Chrissy could be brave in the face of death, then Evan could have courage as he attempted to die to himself—and his own fears.

And yeah, he couldn't control the outcome or how anyone else reacted, but he could take the leap of faith, believing that doing it would make him a better man, whether or not he ever gained anyone else's approval.

CHAPTER 15

Madison's thumb hovered over the send icon. She read and reread the text to Evan. *I'm back, and we need to talk. You free later tonight?*

Was it too cold? Maybe. She'd started with an attempt to lighten the tension sure to be between them. *You still picking me up at nine tonight after your meeting? LOL. Kidding. Unless you are? Either way, we should talk.*

But that had seemed too jovial, making light of the situation.

Man, she was seriously overthinking this. Before she could change her mind altogether about sending the revised text, she did it then slid her phone into the back pocket of her jeans and plopped onto the couch in her aunt's living room.

Madison's eyes locked on her suitcase. Despite her newfound determination to come back to Walker Beach last Friday, she'd stayed in Los Angeles all weekend, working up the courage to return. It wasn't terribly responsible of her to leave the hardware store closed when people might have needed tools and supplies, but they'd been without one for months after Chrissy died, so they could survive an extra week. And since fighting Monday rush-hour traffic out of Los

Angeles this morning, she couldn't force herself to open the store today.

Tomorrow then. And every day thereafter until the store's landlord forced her to close in six or so weeks. After that, who knew? The idea of giving up the hardware store still rankled, still felt a bit like failure, but she'd started to examine her reasons for keeping it. If she were determined to start letting in others, then listening to their advice and insights was part of that. Evan and Ashley had questioned whether the right place for her was the hardware store. Perhaps she should have considered what they'd said instead of immediately refuting it.

What *was* she going to do? Taking in the ocean-themed art on the wall, smelling the eucalyptus in the air, Madison's heart twisted. Could she really sell Aunt Chrissy's house? She definitely didn't need three bedrooms, she could use the money that selling it would bring, and the idea of roommates gave her the heebie-jeebies. Besides, who knew how long it would take to find a job here? She had a text in with Ashley to inquire about the librarian position, but the last time they'd spoken about it her friend had said it might take several months for the job to become available, if ever. Ash wasn't likely to have an update to offer.

No, moving back here was a leap of faith, pure and simple. Because there were no guarantees about so many things—not that Madison would find work she loved or that she'd feel accepted here or even that she'd be able to make things right with Evan.

Definitely no guarantees on that last one.

But this was home. And the only guarantee was that she'd always regret it if she left again.

Enough of all this introspection. She needed to do something, and packing Aunt Chrissy's house was just the thing to keep her mind occupied while she waited for Evan to return her text.

She hauled herself off the couch and pulled out a few garbage bags from under the kitchen sink then walked down the hallway toward the master bedroom. Madison hadn't been in there since returning home, and with one twist of the doorknob, one inhale of Chrissy's favorite essential oil blend, one glance at her lilac bedspread, an unexpected ache overcame her. She slammed the door. Best to tackle that room when her heart wasn't in such a fragile state.

The guest room where Madison had taken up residence since returning home would be the easiest place to start, but she turned instead toward her old bedroom. With a squeak of the door and a flick of the light, she took in the Jane Austen posters on the walls, the muted gray duvet, and the three empty bookcases that told her eighteen-year-old Madison had known she was never coming back.

Rustling bags in hand, she moved inside the room. It was fairly clean already, but surely the closet still contained junk to be sorted. A swing of the door proved Madison's assumption correct, and she started in on the old clothes and shoes that she hadn't worn in years.

The silence threatened to swallow her whole. An audiobook would be a nice way to pass the time. Pulling her phone from her pocket, Madison spied a text from Ashley. *I'm so thrilled you're back! Want to hear more but I've got a full week. The council is voting tonight on the emergency library budget. Will let you know how it pans out. Fingers crossed for the librarian position!*

Madison squatted and rocked back on her heels. OK, then. Maybe she'd know sooner than later.

After flipping on her go-to audio version of *Jane Eyre,* Madison began rifling through boxes, finding mementos from high school. Awards for high academic achievement, dean's list, and the like. Numerous half-finished poems when she'd gone through her beatnik phase. Yearbooks from all four years of high school—each one with only a handful of signatures and KEEP IN TOUCH sentiments strewn throughout.

As she waded through all the memories, her mind kept finding its way back to Evan. A tiny part of her still doubted his sincerity, but the rest of her mind drowned out the doubts. She couldn't help but think about how real he'd seemed each time they'd interacted. The feel of his lips on hers. The way she fit into his arms like she'd been designed for it.

Madison pulled a shoebox from within a larger cardboard box. She opened the lid and gasped, nearly dropping the shoebox. Her eyes blinked in rapid flutters. Was she imagining things?

No, there were the letters from her high school pen pal.

From Evan.

But how? Aunt Chrissy must have saved them when Madison, in her rage, in her heartache, had tossed them into the garbage can ten years ago.

Her hand flew to her mouth at the realization then dove into the box to pick up the letter on top. Skimming at first, still unbelieving, she started to slow down her reading, to take in the words with fresh eyes, to savor each one.

Finally, she reached the last letter, amazed at the vulnerability she'd witnessed so far. But this one ... it stirred her the most.

Dear Secret Pen Pal,

I feel like I need to come up with a different name for you—not because you aren't a secret, because obviously you still are, but because you've become more than a pen pal to me. More than a pal. I hope that's not too weird to say, considering we don't know each other. Although, gotta say, you might know me more than anyone at the moment. How pathetic is that?

Cuz when I write to you, I'm not trying to impress you. I'm not trying to be the perfect son or the perfect friend or the perfect student (although I don't want you to think I'm a complete idiot, so I do double-check that I'm spelling things right, ha ha). But yeah, with you, I can just be . . . I dunno, me, I guess. Sounds totally dumb, but in a world of fakes, this is the one place I can be real. With you.

So, thank you, Mystery Girl.

With that being said, would you want to meet sometime? No pressure. I wouldn't want to meet me after all the stuff I've told you. But maybe?

If that's something that sounds cool to you, then let's meet after school on Friday at Froggies. I'll wear a red baseball hat and have a copy of Pride & Prejudice *in front of me since I know it's your favorite. (Sorry, still haven't read it. Pretty sure I'd lose my man card.)*

Let me know what you think. Again, totally OK if you don't want to do this. Just think about it. I know I'd love to meet you.

Your Maybe-Not-Secret-For-Long Pal

Tears streamed down Madison's face, blotting some of the ink on the page. Lowering the paper, she recalled the way she'd felt when she'd first read Evan's letter. The hope, the thrill, the fear. All of it raced back. She'd contemplated not going. But for the first time in a long time, with the exception of Aunt Chrissy and Ashley, she felt bonded to someone. And she'd desperately wanted to believe it wasn't a lie.

Now, in hindsight, she could see that she'd gone in expecting it to be one. And when it had been Evan, well, that had confirmed all her fears. Had her walls ever been fully lowered? Maybe Madison would have kept her heart protected behind them no matter who had been on the other side of the pen.

In fact, had she even let anyone in but Chrissy since then? Sure, she'd had friends in college and grad school and at the various jobs where she'd worked over the years. But they'd all been surface-level friendships.

Until Evan had coaxed her out of her shell again, giving her a sense of home for the first time since she'd left Walker Beach.

And she'd let her pride get in the way of that. But not anymore.

When her tears were spent and her joints protested at staying in one position for any longer, Madison stood, grimacing as she unwound herself. But nothing was going to stop her from doing what she knew she had to do.

She raced to her old desk, rummaged in the drawer until she found a blank piece of paper, sat, and poised her pen over the page—ready, finally, to say what was in her heart.

And this time, she wasn't holding anything back.

The moment of truth was nearly here. Evan would make his recommendation to the town council. Who knew what would happen after that?

From his spot in the mostly empty audience portion of the council chambers at City Hall, he listened as Ashley presented her request for a line in the library's budget to hire a head librarian in the next month or two.

As she said the words, the ferocity in his dad's eyes laid hard upon him. Evan avoided the mayor's gaze, instead watching his own knee bouncing up and down. Wiping his sweaty palms on the sides of his trousers, Evan inhaled to lower his heart rate.

"Finally, we have also found a location off Ridge Road that could serve as the new library." Ashley tapped her fingers on the speaker's podium as she flew through the details of her presentation. How did she manage to be so poised and at ease? She'd been working hard at this, and a denial from the council would probably feel like a huge setback.

"It's not downtown, so not ideal, but the owner is willing to give it to us for the same price as we were leasing the old building. It's currently empty, so we could sign the lease and move in right away if the council approves it."

Evan ventured a glance up at the council. Bud, Kiki, and Rosa smiled as they jotted a few notes and continued to listen, while Doug scrolled his phone.

And just as he'd suspected, his dad watched Evan. When he caught his eye, Mayor Walsh nodded once. To anyone else, the nod would merely appear as a greeting, an acknowledgment. But Evan knew better.

"That's all I have for now. I'm happy to answer any questions you may have."

Bud adjusted the microphone in front of him—totally unnecessary tonight given the grand total of three people scattered in the audience of the chambers. "I'm all for having an official librarian. Dottie Wildman has done a fabulous job all these years, but you can only expect so much from a volunteer. Hiring a librarian allows us to keep the library open more hours and benefit from someone who has been trained in the latest technology so our services can be expanded. But I'd like to know how you determined the suggested salary for the head librarian."

"Evan Walsh helped with that." Ashley turned around and smiled at him then faced the council once more. "We researched the pay scale for librarians in communities similar to ours and adjusted for the different cost of living in Walker Beach."

Though Dad managed to maintain a neutral face, his eyes took in Evan with a glint of steel.

The other council members bandied more questions before Ashley sat next to Evan.

He leaned toward her. "Great work."

She nudged him with an elbow. "Now go seal the deal."

His stomach twisted at the implication. But it was true. The council would take the recommendation of the community development department into account when making their decision since members were in charge of distributing grant money. And as head community developer, it was up to Evan to inform the board whether or not the funds for the librarian position and library reopening would be available immediately or not.

"And now"—his dad's voice boomed over the speakers, giving him a godlike sound—"head community development officer Evan Walsh will speak to us about the feasibility of the library board's plan based on the funds available as well as make budget recommendations for the second quarter."

Evan stood on weak legs, but he forced one foot in front of the other until he made it to the podium. Swallowing over the lump in his throat, he positioned the speaker's microphone so it would be even with his mouth. "Thank you, Mayor Walsh." A tickle forced a cough from his dry throat.

"The biggest changes take the biggest leaps of faith. And the most courage."

Courage. He held tight to the word. "I agree wholeheartedly with Mr. Travis in his assessment of our town's need for the library. It provides essential services, and it's been closed for far too long already. And a librarian is just what the library needs to function to its maximum efficiency." Evan licked his lips and made eye contact with Dad, who studied him with a veiled look. "That's why I'm recommending the immediate distribution of funds from our town emergency grant fund to give the library exactly what it needs to sign that lease, outfit it, and open its doors as soon as possible."

"If we use those funds for the library, won't that leave a few other businesses without the funds necessary to survive and thrive?" His dad's question pounded into Evan one word at a time, and he didn't miss the slight snarl beginning to curve the mayor's lips.

Evan straightened his shoulders. He needed to say everything he had to say tonight because who knew if he'd have a job tomorrow? "I've been meeting regularly with all the business owners in town who have requested grants through the proper channels, and I've already expedited small grants to those most in need of our town's help to survive the lagging economy. The others either have not been affected or have a windfall sufficient to protect them from bankruptcy in the time being. I stand firmly behind my recommendation."

His father sat back in his chair without another word—but if he'd been Superman, his glare would have melted Evan's flesh.

And for a long time, he *had* been Superman, in Evan's eyes at least. The crash-and-burn of his respect for his dad still stung.

Evan finished giving his recommendations then took a seat next to Ashley, whose huge grin reassured him he'd controlled the only thing he could—his own actions. As soon as the meeting adjourned, Evan stood. He'd forgotten his phone in his office drawer and needed to grab it before he left for home. Once he was in his office, he strode to his desk.

The door slammed behind him, and he turned.

His dad stood there, fists clenched at his side. "Just what was that all about, Evan?"

Evan leaned against his desk, attempting a casual stance while the pounding blood in his veins told him he was anything but. "I'm sorry you don't agree with the recommendation, Dad. But it was the right thing to do."

"The right—" His dad grunted. "Do you know what this recommendation will cost me?"

"No, but that's not my concern. I'm doing my job. I never signed up to be a politician."

"And you'll never be one now. You can forget winning the bid for councilman after this."

"I didn't want it anyway." Evan was questioning if he even wanted to stay in his current job. While he liked working toward a better Walker Beach, he recognized now that he'd taken the job to impress his dad. All weekend long, Bud's exhortation for Evan to continue fighting for what he wanted had led to second-guessing everything he'd once believed. If he were to choose a career based solely on what made *him* happy, what would it be?

He still didn't have an answer, but he was finally asking the question.

Dad's eyes turned downward, and he allowed the snarl to fully come out now that they were in private. "I'm disappointed in you, son."

"I'm sorry to hear that. I wish you'd respect me for the fact I won't be manipulated, that I've become a man capable of making my own decisions. But I'm finally able to respect myself, and that's what really matters." He turned, glimpsed a paper on his desk, and snatched it up. He'd planned to address this with his dad tomorrow, but suddenly his discovery just before the council meeting didn't seem like something he wanted to wait on. "I'm glad you're here, though. There's something I want to talk to you about."

Striding closer, his dad took the paper from his hand, eyes widening as he read. "What is this?"

"I contacted Carol Davenport about her sudden decision to not renew Madison's lease. After some persuasion, she decided to do the right thing. Says you called her and asked for a favor as an 'old friend.' That right there is her written account of what happened."

"You can't believe everything you read." His dad crumpled the paper and shoved it into his pocket.

"I have the email still, so I can print another copy." The tension in Evan's temple increased as his teeth clenched. "And it would be easy to forward to Piper Lansbury over at *The Walker Beach Press,* should the things mentioned in that letter not be reversed. Immediately."

Yep, there was the large vein popping from Dad's forehead,

the telltale sign that Evan had better watch out. But he wasn't a child anymore, and Dad couldn't take his belt to him. Sure, he could fire Evan, and he could tarnish his reputation. But Evan was tired of cowering.

"Are you threatening me?"

"Basically."

The fists at Dad's sides were back, and his rapid inhales echoed in the room. But then he got eerily calm. Removed his jacket, laid it across Alex's desk, rolled up his sleeves, smiled. "You're just confused, Evan. That girl, she has you confused."

"Madison and I broke up, Dad." At least, he assumed that's what her silence and her fleeing Walker Beach meant. "This is about me doing the right thing, even when the guy who was supposed to teach me that failed at his responsibility."

"You are way out of line here."

"No, you are. And if I don't hear that Carol has offered Madison an extended contract by the end of business tomorrow, then I will be forwarding that message to Piper."

"What about Herman Hardware? Our agreement was based on the knowledge that there would be no competition."

"That's unfortunate but it doesn't change my mind about what's right."

"But you agreed that it was better for the economy. Think about what you're doing, son."

"For once, I am. And I'm deciding to let the chips fall where they may. If Herman decides to cancel the contract, so be it. If they decide to stay and fight, I'll help Madison fight harder."

"You're betraying your town. Your family."

"No, Dad. You did that when you took a morally ambiguous road to get what you wanted." Evan maneuvered toward his desk drawer, lifted his phone from inside, and strode toward the door. "Good night, Mayor Walsh."

Then he headed to his truck without stopping.

After sliding into his seat, he leaned back against the headrest and closed his eyes. When his heart rate slowed a couple of minutes later, he loosened and removed his tie, flinging it onto the passenger's seat.

His phone vibrated on the center console, and he picked it up. A text message from Ashley, probably thanking him again for tonight.

But wait. Below that, his eyes caught sight of a message he must have missed from earlier today. Not surprising since he'd kept his phone stuffed away while he'd been glued to his computer in preparation for the meeting. And yeah, he also hadn't liked staring at the date at the top of the screen. As much as he was not a Hallmark holiday kind of guy, he'd been planning a really great Valentine's Day for him and Madison, and canceling their reservations had nearly killed him.

When he swiped to open the text message, he straightened in his seat. It was from Madison, and she'd asked if he was free tonight. Right now.

And he'd ignored it. Or that's what she'd think, anyway.

He held back a curse and typed in a response right away. *Sorry, just saw this. I'm free now if you are?*

Then he stared at the phone, waiting and praying for three little dots to pop up, proof that she was responding.

But nothing happened.

Should he head to her house anyway? What if she was asleep? Or mad that he hadn't answered?

As he was pulling out from the parking lot, still unsure of which way he was going to turn, his phone vibrated again. Scooping it up, he took in the message. *Come on over.*

She didn't have to tell him twice. He gunned it down the street toward her house, parked, and leaped out. Probably looked desperate, but he didn't care. He'd thought they were over, but maybe . . .

When he got there, his fingers moved to ring the bell. But some sort of note was taped over it. The outside read *To My Not-So-Secret Pen Pal*. He fumbled to remove the note from the bell.

His hands shook as he read. Then he hightailed it back to his truck, got in, and sped away.

CHAPTER 16

Madison's fingers were nearly frozen through.

And no wonder. The temp tonight was in the forties, and the circulating air off the ocean was particularly cold. She'd huddled under the blanket she'd thrown in her car at the last minute. Of course, she wasn't the only one at the park who'd dreamed up a late-night Valentine's rendezvous, as evidenced by the number of cars in the parking lot and the small fires going all over the beach. But she'd bet she was the only one all by herself.

Maybe he wasn't going to show after all.

"What did you expect, Madison? For him to rush back to you after you left without a word?" Yeah, she probably sounded crazy talking to herself, but moving her lips and exhaling air warmed her.

And made her feel not quite so alone.

But no. Even if Evan decided not to come tonight, she wasn't alone. She had all the people who had made Walker Beach a home, and whatever came next, she would lean into them in the days to come.

Her rear had grown numb from the cold seeping through

the rocks off Baker Community Park. She'd contemplated a number of spots to ask Evan to meet her, like the baseball diamond where they'd shared their first kiss, but this had seemed the most appropriate. Because this was where she'd first decided to really and truly trust him.

And now this was where she was going to ask him to trust her.

If he ever showed up.

Madison blew into her hands to spread her inner warmth outward. "Why did you have to come so early?" Two hours ago, in fact. She'd known he wouldn't even be out of his weekly meeting until at least eight-thirty, but seven o'clock had rolled around, and she couldn't wait at home any longer.

Of course, there had been the possibility that he wouldn't find her note at all. But she'd clung to her faith in him, her faith in what they had, and she'd come anyway. Now that he'd probably found it, what would he think? What would he do?

At least the full moon overhead kept her company.

The sound of crunching rocks drew her attention to the right, and she gulped the sudden anxiety clawing at her throat. Evan crested the hill, hands clutching a white paper that shone against the darkness overhead. When he caught sight of her, he stopped—and so did her breath.

"Hey." Her throat contracted, turning her greeting into an imitation of Kermit the Frog. Madison told her legs to stand, but she couldn't force herself to do so. Her fingers curled tighter as she gripped the blanket around her shoulders.

"Did you mean this?" He waved the note in the air as he advanced, lowering himself to the sand-littered ground beside her despite his dress pants.

Madison bit her lip. "Yes."

Evan stared at her for a moment then shook his head. "Even this part?" He grabbed his phone and turned on the flashlight, illuminating the paper in front of him as he read out loud. *"I've spent a lot of years trying to get by on my own because I didn't want the pain when someone inevitably let me down. But I'm learning that people can still surprise me, if I give them the opportunity to do so. You surprised me, Evan. The love I feel for you surprised me. I didn't want to love you, but how could I not, when you're such a good man? But not just good in a general sense—though you are that. But you're also good for me."*

He cleared his throat as he lowered the paper and set his phone aside then looked at her again.

She allowed the blanket to fall, leaving her torso exposed to the elements. Despite the sweatshirt she wore, a biting wind blew through her. But it wouldn't stop her from saying what she needed to say. Madison reached her hand toward Evan's, grateful when he didn't pull away. "Yes, especially that part." She wound their fingers together, and he didn't resist. "Evan, I'm sorry for leaving town without talking to you. I was hurt, but that was no excuse. My leaving probably made you feel like you didn't matter. But you mattered too much."

"What do you mean?"

"Ever since my parents died, I retreated from people—real ones, anyway. The fictional ones gave and gave, never requiring anything of me." She stuck her tongue out to make fun of herself. "I told myself that if I let people get close to me, they could leave me, disappoint me, hurt me. And that's actually all true. That's why I ran—because I didn't know how to handle the fact I'd slipped and let you in."

Evan looked like he might protest but didn't say anything. A squeeze to her hand encouraged her to go on.

"But I was forgetting something my Aunt Chrissy taught me. That the best relationships are worth any heartache and pain they may bring." She leaned closer. "You are worth it, Evan Walsh. And no matter how you feel about me, I just had to tell you that. And that I love you."

A smile split Evan's face. "Then I guess I should tell you that

I love you too." With his free hand, he took a strand of her hair and rubbed it between his thumb and forefinger. Then, slowly, he slid his fingers all the way into her hair and gently tugged her closer, tilting her face toward his. Lowering his mouth, he met her lips in a sweet kiss that held such promise she wanted to weep.

Evan pulled back, touching her nose to his for a moment before sitting up straighter. "Now that we have that out of the way . . ."

She laughed.

So did he but then he sobered. "I need to tell you I'm sorry. I didn't stand up for you like I should have. I was just so desperate for my father's approval, but I pretty much ruined any chance I have of that tonight. And yet, I've never been prouder of myself."

Madison quirked an eyebrow. "What did you do?"

First, he secured the blanket around them both. Then told her about his recommendation that the emergency grant money go toward the library—and a new library director position. The thought squeezed her heart. "And I may have also said I'd tell Piper Lansbury about Dad's hand in your canceled lease if he didn't get it called off."

"What?"

Evan nodded as his thumb stroked the palm of her hand. "He was the one who arranged the whole thing. Dad and Carol dated in high school, and he knew some things about her that she wouldn't want getting out there come reunion time. She wouldn't tell me what exactly, but . . ."

"Wow." How sad. Then a thought occurred to her. "Wait. So what did he say to your, uh, suggestion?"

"You can call it a threat. It was." Evan peered deep into her eyes. "I will threaten anyone who tries to hurt the woman I love."

She nearly melted into him. But there was one more thing she needed to know. "So . . ."

"Oh, right. He didn't say anything, but we'll know for sure tomorrow. I'm pretty confident his good name means more to him than *anything* else though." He paused. "Which means that you can keep your store open. I know it may be hard to compete with Herman Hardware, if they decide to not void the agreement, but I've already been thinking about ways we can campaign for business. People love local, so I'm sure we can play to that."

"I thought you said that I should be a librarian." She teased but she really did want to know. Had his thoughts on the matter changed?

"It doesn't matter what I think. I want to support you. Isn't that what you do when you love someone?" He kissed her cheek, her earlobe, then trailed kisses up her jaw until he reached the side of her mouth. "And if I wasn't clear before, let me repeat it. I love you, Madison Price."

She threw her arms around this man who had proven he would fight for her, no matter what. "And I love you, Evan Walsh. My hero."

EPILOGUE

TWO MONTHS LATER

The day was finally here.

Madison flit from one corner of the place to another, straightening art that didn't need to be straightened and picking imaginary lint off the ground. Her heels clacked on the wood floors as she ran to the restroom, looking herself over in the mirror one more time. Hair tucked into a loose bun at the base of her neck and glasses on her face, along with a crisp white collared shirt and a pair of gray trousers left her "looking the part," as Evan had said this morning when he'd arrived to help.

She shivered as she remembered the look in his eye that stated he liked what he saw.

Shoving thoughts of him from her mind, she straightened her shoulders and strode out of the swinging bathroom door. Her all-volunteer staff waited near the large wraparound circulation desk, which sat in the middle of the rows and rows of shelves. They'd painted the place a cheery butter yellow, which made the ceilings appear higher than they were and brightened it in a new way.

As he chatted with Ashley, Evan lounged in the seat behind

the desk, his feet propped up on the counter. Between his work, festival preparations, and online school—he'd decided to pursue being a high school physical education teacher, a job that would allow him to coach baseball one day—they'd had to fight for time together. But every moment was better than the last.

When he saw her, he scrambled upward. "Your throne, Your Majesty."

Madison rolled her eyes and swatted him. "I'm no queen."

"But this *is* your kingdom." His eyes sparkled as he planted a kiss on her cheek.

Her cheeks burned at the public display. After all, this was her place of work. But looking around at the volunteers—Mrs. Wildman, Bud and Velma Travis, Ashley and her cousin Shannon, Ben, Bella, Alex, Evan—she knew it was also her home.

"I like the sound of that." Madison squeezed Evan's hand then turned to face the group. "All right, people, the day has finally arrived. The reopening of the newly christened Chrissy Price Public Library is upon us."

As she said the words, she nearly cried. It had been Evan's idea to name the place after her aunt, especially since they'd decided to convert her former hardware store into the library. Carol Davenport had offered to donate the space to the city, which had allowed them to use the extra funds to add thousands of wonderful books to the collection of those that had survived the earthquake. Madison had spent days in here, sorting, cataloging, and shelving each book with love, even sending prayers of hope for those who would read the pages she'd held in her hands.

"Thank you again for your countless hours given to this effort. With all the programs we've put into place, I just know our community is going to thrive."

The residents of Walker Beach weren't the only ones thriving. Madison herself had blossomed since she'd decided to close the hardware store and interview for the library director position—to embrace the dream she'd had for her life. After all, Chrissy had only ever wanted her to be happy and whole. And though she would have accepted the job even if it had been funded with grant money, the fact it was built into the city's future budget made the job that much more appealing.

Madison looked toward the front doors, where a line of people already gathered on this bright and sunny Thursday in April. "Let's do this!" She sank into the chair behind her computer.

Ashley joined her. Other than helping at the library here and there, her friend hadn't been around much, and Madison took a good look at her. Though she was as stylish and friendly as ever on the surface, there appeared to be an underlying strain in Ashley's eyes. A worry, something that interfered with her friend's laid-back nature.

"You all right?"

"Hmm?" Ashley's eyes remained fixed on the doors, which Evan would unlock in precisely three minutes. "Oh, yeah. I'm fine. Just tired. Lots of work and such."

"You sure that's it?"

Biting her lip, Ashley turned her head toward Madison. "Derek's coming back this weekend."

"Derek?"

"Derek Campbell."

As in, the guy Ashley had been half in love with in junior high and high school? "Wasn't he best friends with Ben growing up?"

Her friend played with a strand of her long hair. "Yeah."

"Where has he been?"

"He left for Europe fourteen months ago to work at a vineyard. Kind of an internship opportunity. Before he went, we got . . . close."

"Did you date?"

"What? No. Nothing like that." Ashley sighed. "I thought, for a while, that maybe he saw me as more than his best friend's little sister, maybe even more than a friend, but he never said anything. And then he left, and it's been really hard to connect. He's busy, I'm busy. We just . . . have been living different lives. I haven't spoken to him in forever. I only know he's coming back because I ran into his dad at the market."

"It's always hard when we drift apart from the ones we love." Madison placed a hand over Ashley's. "Did you ever tell him how you felt about him?"

Ashley's sharp look revealed the truth in Madison's question. Then, after a moment's hesitation, she swallowed. "No. But . . . maybe. I don't know. Maybe I will."

"You should." Peeking up at Evan, Madison smiled. He watched her, waiting. She gave the thumbs-up sign, and he turned to unlock the front door. Then she turned back to Ashley. "You never know what will happen when you kick down your walls and open your heart to love."

And as the door swung wide, people streamed into the library, and Madison embraced the incoming flood with joyful arms.

Want more? Access a bonus epilogue with just a bit more of Evan and Madison's happily ever after on my Reader Freebies page at www.lindsayharrel.com/reader-freebies.

CONNECT WITH LINDSAY

Thanks so much for joining Evan and Madison on their journey! I hope you loved them as much as I do. If so, would you mind doing me a favor and leaving a review on Goodreads, Bookbub, or your favorite retail site?

I'd love to connect with you. Sign up for my newsletter at www.lindsayharrel.com/subscribe and I'll send you a FREE story as a thank you!

Can't get enough of Walker Beach? You can read Ashley's story in the next book, *All I've Waited For.* Turn the page for a sneak peek...

ALL I'VE WAITED FOR SNEAK PEEK

Life these days was a never-ending sprint.

Good thing Ashley Baker liked to run.

Her feet pounded the wooden boardwalk and music poured through her AirPods as she wove around people out for a leisurely stroll along the Pacific Ocean's edge. In the distance, seagulls lazily dipped toward the water. Neighborhood children built sandcastles, their parents watching from the shade of a nearby umbrella. The seventy-degree sun and clear skies had lured townspeople of all generations out to enjoy this late-April Saturday in Walker Beach, California, the small town nestled off Highway 1 between Los Angeles and San Francisco where Ashley had lived her entire life.

How tempting it was to join them.

But Kyle Mahaney, her boss, would kill Ashley if she arrived late to their new clients' meeting at Whimsical Weddings & More. He'd even asked her to come a few minutes earlier than usual, which had meant cutting short the planning meeting for this summer's Baker family reunion. Thankfully it only took seven and a half minutes to jog from her parents' house to the downtown office.

Ashley's music halted as a call came through her phone, which was tucked in the back pocket of her jeans. Slowing to a brisk walk, she answered the call. "Ashley here."

"Hey, cuz."

"Hi." Normally, she'd love to chat with Shannon. But not right now. "Sorry, I only have like two seconds."

"So what's new?" An easy laugh filled the line, and Ashley pictured her cousin's bright eyes and winsome smile. They looked more like sisters than cousins, both tan with long blonde hair—although at nearly six feet, Ashley stood a half-foot taller. And, while Ashley's build was more athletic in nature, Shannon's delicate features matched her artistic spirit well. "You're always busy."

"Yeah, yeah." What could she say? Ashley loved planning events and she loved people, so when there was a chance to volunteer for something events related, she almost always said yes.

Staying busy also had the happy advantage of keeping her mind off of less pleasant things.

The sea lapped along the shore, sparkling under the midday Californian sun. "So, what's up?"

"Just wondering if you'd seen him yet."

Ashley nearly groaned at the reminder. "He's only been back in town for a day."

Stepping off the boardwalk, she took the intersecting sidewalk to Main Street in the North Village. This part of town had experienced damage from an earthquake nine months ago, and some businesses had never recovered. Thankfully, Kyle's business hadn't been one of them, and Ashley's job had remained secure.

"What's he waiting for? Your house should've been his first stop."

"I don't think anyone else has seen him either." Ashley only knew Derek Campbell was back because earlier this week his dad, Jack, had informed her of his impending return. The thought still tightened her throat. "Haven't heard anything from the Walker Beach gossips, anyway."

"But you're going to tell him how you feel when you see him, right?"

"It's been over a year since he left. Things are bound to be different between us."

"No way. You guys had something special even though neither of you ever said anything."

A sigh filtered across the airwaves. With all of Shannon's romantic notions, it was a wonder that she'd never had a boyfriend. Probably had something to do with feeling stuck in her older sister Quinn's shadow—and her extreme shyness when it came to any male their age that she wasn't related to.

"You deserve to be happy, Ash. Just promise me you'll think about it, okay?"

Shannon was never pushy. This obviously meant a lot to her.

"Okay, okay. *If* he ever comes to see me." Ashley flitted past a few shoppers and finally reached the pale pink storefront where she worked. The front window display—which Shannon had helped design a year ago when Ashley had started her job here—showed off a lovely A-line wedding dress with see-through sleeves and intricate beading on the bodice. A ladder shelf created a pretty hodgepodge of wedding-themed elements, from a large wooden Mr. & Mrs. to hurricane vases, soft pink candles, and paper lanterns. "Sorry, Shan, I've gotta go. I'll see you tomorrow night at Family Dinner, right?"

"Of course. I'd never risk the wrath of the Baker Matrons."

Ashley laughed in response as she opened the door and a bell rang overhead. "I always knew you were smart."

They said goodbye and Ashley strode through the small showroom that exhibited scrapbooks, sample wedding invitations, and a whole wall of framed photos featuring gorgeous brides of all shapes and colors with one thing in common—their faces shone with love.

And each one had a man who loved them back.

She turned her head and kept walking until she reached Kyle's office in the back. "Knock, knock."

Her boss looked up from his tidy desk. "Ah, come in, Ashley, come in." The room smelled of coconut, probably from the sunscreen Kyle wore religiously ever since his wife, Cathy, had died of skin cancer ten years ago.

"I hope I'm not late." She slid into the overstuffed chair on the other side of the desk, sinking into the plush maroon cushions. Her muscles relaxed even if her brain couldn't. Kyle hadn't said why he wanted to meet early. Ashley had wracked her brain all day trying to think of something she'd missed, but other than a minor miscommunication with one of their brides that Kyle had cleaned up, she couldn't think of anything.

"No, we have a few minutes until our appointment." Kyle leaned back in his chair and fiddled with the end of his white handlebar mustache. With his Harley-Davidson jean vest, cowboy hat covering a bald head, and wide girth, he was the very opposite of what one would picture as a wedding planner. But this business had been his wife's dream, and when she'd passed, he'd quit his job as a trucker and taken up her mantle, whipping up some of the most fabulous events Walker Beach had ever seen.

"Great. So, what did you want to talk about?" Ashley crossed her legs, then uncrossed them again.

"The future." Kyle sighed. "I'm getting older, and as you know, the pace of this business can be stressful. Hiring you on has helped tremendously, but I've found myself more and more ready for a rest."

Ashley released a whoosh of air. Nothing she'd done wrong, then. "I understand needing a vacation." Kyle always seemed to have everything well in hand, but she really wasn't surprised by his stress level given his business's success and the way he held tight to the reins—even those he'd given Ashley charge over. "Are you planning to go soon? I can handle the Whitman wedding and the Dreyfuss anniversary party on my own, no problem."

"No, Ashley. What I'm saying is that I've decided to retire."

"What? When?"

"In about two months. Late June sometime."

"I see." Her days wouldn't be the same without him here. Kyle could be gruff at times, and he expected a lot from her, but really he was just a big softie underneath all that bluster.

But wait. What was she thinking? This was *his* company. "What's going to happen to the business?" Was she about to be out of a job?

Or maybe ... maybe the chance to live out her childhood dreams was finally here.

For years, Ashley had wanted to start her own wedding planning business. After getting a bachelor's in event management online while busing tables at Froggies—her aunt and uncle's pizza parlor and arcade—she'd worked as an assistant event planner for the city of Walker Beach. A great experience, but she'd always longed to focus on weddings. So when Kyle had opened a position at Whimsical Weddings, she'd jumped at the chance and had loved every minute there.

Sure, she'd do some things differently than he did, and yes, she wished Kyle would trust her to handle some weddings by herself. But the chance to help brides have the most perfect day ever ... well, that was right up Ashley's alley. This job had been a fabulous jumping-off point for that. Yet still her desire lingered, tucked away in the corner of her heart for some time in the future when she had the time, energy, and money to devote to it.

But maybe "the future" was now.

Ashley leaned forward in anticipation of Kyle's response.

He scratched his chin and looked away from her, studying the potted succulent in the corner of the room. It had started blooming since she'd last been in here, its baby pink flowers barely open. Ashley had given it to Kyle on the last anniversary of his wife's death.

"Cathy started this company thirty years ago, you know. She built it from the ground up, and it meant the world to her." His voice always went soft when he spoke of his wife.

"I know." Cathy, who had been friends with her parents, was one of the kindest, gentlest souls Ashley had ever met.

"She always talked about leaving the business to our children, but ..." Kyle cleared his throat.

Somehow, she remembered overhearing Cathy and Mom talking on the couch one day when Ashley was about ten. Cathy had cried and cried over yet another failed adoption.

Now, Ashley resisted the urge to cross the room and hug Kyle. Her boss probably wouldn't appreciate the sympathy, which he would undoubtedly interpret as pity. "What's your plan, then?" They may not be related by blood, but Kyle was a mentor to her, someone she trusted to steer her in the right direction in more than just business, and she'd like to think he thought of her as a kind of daughter—or at the very least, as a friend.

Were they on the same page? Was Kyle going to leave her the business?

Ashley gripped the sides of her chair, her stomach fluttering.

"I have a niece in San Francisco. She's always been interested in event planning. Even interned with us several years back."

The words punched Ashley in the gut. "Oh." It was a miracle she could get the response past her lips.

"Are you all right? You look pale."

"I'm fine." What could she say? He had every right to do what he wanted with his business. "So, you've asked her then? She wants to move here and take it over?"

Frowning, he lifted the hat off his head and fanned himself. "Not yet, no. But I plan to go up and see my sister tomorrow, and her daughter will be there. Thought it better to talk about in person."

So Ashley still had a shot—but should she take it? Cathy had wanted to keep the business in the family, and Ashley should respect that. She'd just let it go. "I hope the conversation goes well."

Kyle's hawk eyes studied her. "And if she doesn't want it, well …"

Ashley's gaze collided with his. "You aren't going to close the business, are you?" He couldn't, wouldn't, not when it had meant so much to Cathy.

Not when it meant so much to Ashley—the chance it represented, anyway.

"I don't know that I have a choice." Kyle folded his hands over his stomach. "Not unless …"

Somehow Ashley had scooted to the front edge of her seat. "Unless what?"

"Unless there was someone else who wanted it."

"Yes!" Ashley felt her eyes widen at the intensity of her declaration and she clapped a hand over her mouth.

Kyle chuckled. "So you might be interested in buying me out?"

Her chest deflated. "I don't have the funds to do that." Maybe she could get a business loan, though. Something. "But if you give me a chance to look into it, I'd be interested." She paused. "Very interested. It … it would be a dream, actually."

"Is this some whim or something you've thought about before?"

"I never really thought about taking over your business, necessarily. I've been content to just learn from you. But yes, I've wanted to own a wedding planning business since I can remember." Ashley placed a hand flat on the desk. "And I'd be honored to continue Cathy's legacy, even if I'm not a Mahaney."

"I believe you would." Back and forth Kyle swiveled ever so slightly in his desk chair, the wheels emitting a low squeak. "And regarding the money, I'd be fine with a slow purchase. You could pay me over the course of five years, or maybe we'd go into it as partners—you doing the labor, and me as an investor of sorts, until your portion was paid."

What a kind man. What an opportunity. "That is so generous."

Kyle's eyes narrowed a bit. "It's still business. With this solution, I'd actually be paid for the business, which is more than I'd get if I left it to my niece."

"Of course." Ashley bit her lip to hold back a grin. The teddy bear was hiding behind the grizzly's teeth, but she knew better.

"I'm serious, young lady." Kyle tilted his head. "The money isn't a concern to me, but the legacy part is. And I do have some concerns about your ability to handle it."

Really? Ashley had been nothing but helpful and competent. She couldn't help but feel the nip of his words. "In what way?"

"Your level of experience, for one. And your schedule for another. You're busy all the time."

"So are you."

"Yes, but mine is mostly business related. You're always running from one meeting to another. First, you were on the library board—"

"Which I've stepped down from." Her friend Madison had recently taken over as Walker Beach's head librarian, so Ashley hadn't felt the town needed her as much anymore.

"Yes, but what else have you added? You're overseeing the town's committee for the Christmas festival—"

"The community development officer personally asked if I'd do that. And the whole idea of the festival is for the town to band together and revitalize our economy after the earthquake harmed it."

"I know, Ashley. I'm on the committee too, remember?"

"Right." She shouldn't get so defensive.

"And aren't you also coordinating your family's reunion this summer? Not to mention taking on extra responsibilities and saying yes to everyone who asks something of you. Cumulatively, it's a lot, and adding the ownership of a business might be too much. You're used to having my help with every event, and you've had me to fall back on when you weren't sure about something. But if I retire and it's all on your shoulders ... well, I don't want you to flounder."

He didn't believe she could do this? "I don't want that either."

"Your heart is in the right place. I just want to be sure you can actually handle this before you've got money invested and Cathy's legacy is put in danger."

"I'd never want that either." Ashley furrowed her brow. "How can I prove to you that I've got this?"

The bell jangled from the showroom.

Kyle glanced at the clock on the wall. "It's about time for our appointment. We'll have to continue this conversation later." He gathered his planner, then paused. His lips twisted to the side. "You know, this couple has asked for a very quick turnaround. They want to be married Memorial Day weekend."

Ashley's jaw fell. "That's only six weeks away."

"I know, but they were desperate and didn't blink at the premium I quoted for the rush. And Moonstone Lodge happens to be available on the date in question."

"Wow, really?" She straightened. Where was he going with this? "Okay."

"You asked how you can prove yourself to me. Take on this wedding all by yourself. I'll stay completely out of it. You run the show. If you can pull it off with everything else you have going on, you'll demonstrate that this is important enough to you. We'll work out the other ownership details later if it goes well. How does that sound?"

Ashley squealed and leaped from her seat, rounding the desk and throwing her arms around Kyle's neck. "I say you've got yourself a deal."

"Settle down or our clients will think we're hiding a pig back here."

Laughing, Ashley kissed him on the cheek and stole his planner from him. "I'll take that. You just stay here and relax. Or better yet, go out and enjoy the sunshine."

"Maybe I will."

With pep in her step, Ashley closed his door behind her and paused, adrenaline working its way through her whole system. As she entered the showroom, she caught sight of a tall brunette perusing the photo wall. The woman looked up, and Ashley was struck by her large blue eyes.

She held out her hand. "Hi, there. I'm Ashley Baker, your wedding planner."

The woman, who wore a couture black-and-white tie-neck blouse and pencil skirt, returned her shake. "Claire Boivin. My fiancé will be here in a moment. He's parking the car."

"You have a lovely accent." Ashley smiled warmly. "Do you live nearby?"

"*Non,* I'm from France. My fiancé lives here, though." Claire arched an eyebrow. "I believe I spoke with a man on the phone, *oui?*" She walked toward the silk flower display and began flipping through the book of photos.

From her movements to her dainty nose, thin lips, and smooth pale skin, this woman oozed elegance and grace. In Ashley's experience, brides like her were typically high maintenance with unrealistic expectations, but that didn't fit with someone whose planning timetable was so short. Or Ashley hoped so, anyway. It would be challenging enough to pull together something small and simple, but if the woman desired a blowout bash, well … Ashley wasn't going to sleep for the next six weeks.

Still, it would be worth it to finally own the business of her dreams.

She followed Claire to the display. "Yes, that was my boss, Kyle. He's appointed me as the lead planner, and I'm very excited to make your dreams come true."

Claire nodded, apparently satisfied.

They both turned as the bell chimed. Ashley's eyes widened at the tall man with broad shoulders who entered.

Derek had finally come to see her.

She rushed toward him, trying to still her shaking hands. Oh man, he looked good, better than she remembered. His brown hair was swept back in an Elvis cut, and his skin had bronzed, probably from so much time in the French vineyards. He'd grown a beard, and though Ashley wasn't normally one for facial hair, it suited him.

"Hi. It's so good to see you." She lowered her voice. "I'm with a client right now, but I'd love to catch up. Can I meet you for coffee in about an hour?"

Derek stared at Ashley as if he'd never seen her before, his deep brown eyes crinkling at the corners. "Ashley? What are you doing here?"

As if he'd slapped her, she took a step back. "What do you m—"

"Derek? Do you two know each other?"

Ashley froze. Her eyes moved from Derek to Claire, blinking rapidly. Understanding dawned as Claire joined them, each click of her heels on tile punctuating the truth.

Derek wasn't here to see Ashley.

Well, he was. Just not in the way she'd dreamed about.

"You're …" She cleared her throat. "You're the groom?"

He averted his eyes, swinging his head toward Claire, who smiled at him. "I am."

No. No, no, no.

Ashley forced a smile. "Would you excuse me for a moment?" Then she turned and bolted toward the back as gracefully as she could.

Kyle would have to take this wedding. She couldn't do it.

Reaching for the doorknob, she twisted it, but her hand was too slick with sweat to get it the first time. Finally, she managed to open the door.

Kyle didn't glance up from the bridal magazine he was reading. "Did our experiment fail already?" He licked his finger and turned the page.

Ashley grimaced. What was she doing in here? She couldn't give up her dream opportunity. Not over a guy who hadn't bothered to call one of his supposed best friends more than once after he'd gone overseas fourteen months ago.

Over someone who had gotten engaged and hadn't bothered to let her know.

"Not at all." Her gaze tumbled over Kyle's desk until she caught sight of a random checklist. Ashley swooped in and grabbed it. "Just needed this."

Without waiting to gauge Kyle's reaction, she left the office as quickly as she'd come in.

Before she entered the showroom again, she stopped and took a deep breath. Yeah, this was going to be awkward, but she could do it. She'd likely be working mostly with Claire anyway, and she'd just try to forget that Derek was the groom.

Try to forget how, despite his distance and the way he'd acted like their friendship—like she—meant nothing to him, Ashley Baker was still in love with him.

Oh boy.

She steeled her spine and walked into the room. "All right, ya'll, let's get this wedding planned!"

BOOKS BY LINDSAY HARREL

Walker Beach Romance Series

All At Once (prequel novella)

All of You, Always

All Because of You

All I've Waited For

All You Need Is Love

Port Willis Series

The Secrets of Paper and Ink

Like a Winter Snow

Like a Christmas Dream

Standalones

The Joy of Falling

The Heart Between Us

One More Song to Sing

ABOUT THE AUTHOR

Lindsay Harrel is a lifelong book nerd who lives in Arizona with her young family and two golden retrievers in serious need of training. When she's not writing or chasing after her children, Lindsay enjoys making a fool of herself at Zumba, curling up with anything by Jane Austen, and savoring sour candy one piece at a time. Visit her at www.lindsayharrel.com.

facebook.com/lindsayharrel

instagram.com/lindsayharrelauthor

Walker Beach Romance Series

Book 2: All Because of You

Published by Blue Aster Press

Cover: Hillary Manton Lodge Design

Editing: Marisa Deshaies

CPSIA information can be obtained
at www.ICGtesting.com
Printed in the USA
LVHW092036080421
683868LV00006B/1143

9 781736 194430